RIVER OF REVENGE

Pretty archaeologist Lucy Luffy and Professor Matt Strangeways are searching for brontosaurus remains in Colorado, but their problems start when they lose all their equipment in the Flaming Gorge. Jesse Greer's thieving gang, Luke Greaves — the greasy sheriff of Dutch John — and rebellious Ute Indians accelerate the pair's troubles. Can bounty hunter Jim Roland catch up with Greer and his gang after they kidnap Lucy? And can Lucy hang on to her life, or even her virtue?

JOHN DYSON

RIVER OF REVENGE

Complete and Unabridged

LINFORD
Leicester

First published in Great Britain in 2004 by
Robert Hale Limited
London

First Linford Edition
published 2006
by arrangement with
Robert Hale Limited
London

British Library CIP Data

Dyson, John, *1943 –*
    River of revenge.—Large print ed.—
Linford western library
1. Western stories
2. Large type books
I. Title
823.9'14 [F]

ISBN 1–84617–129–6

Published by
F. A. Thorpe (Publishing)
Anstey, Leicestershire

Set by Words & Graphics Ltd.
Anstey, Leicestershire
Printed and bound in Great Britain by
T. J. International Ltd., Padstow, Cornwall

This book is printed on acid-free paper

1

'Oh, my God!' Lucy Luffy licked her dry lips apprehensively as she saw the white water looming up, splashing and gurgling upon black rocks sharp as sharks' fins. At that moment it struck her they were in danger of losing everything they possessed, even their lives. 'You didn't warn us it was going to be like this.'

George Dowson, the riverman at whom she screamed the words, hung onto the pine pole rudder-stick of his raft, his weatherbeaten face immobile beneath the peak of his Dutchman's hat, his eyes, through narrowed lids, scanning the approach to Flaming Gorge. 'Hang on,' he shouted.

That, it seemed, was all they could do as they were swept onwards by the smooth, strong sheen of the Green River in a dreadful silence that was transformed gradually into a dull, threatening roar as the river poured into the narrow, sheer-walled gorge. One thing was for sure: there was no going back.

The raft began to buck and twist on the powerful whirligig of current and the knuckles of her companion, Dr Matthew Strangeways, whitened as he took the boatman's advice and knelt down, gripping his fists around a spar. Was this to be the end of all their efforts and preparations?

Strangeways had not wanted to come at first. A dark-haired, intense man nearing middle years, he had been content in the fusty filing rooms of the Chicago Archaeological Museum before the young blue-stocking, Miss Luffy, had talked him into this crazy adventure. What was he doing on this roped-together pile of logs being carried towards imminent danger?

They had worked together at the museum cataloguing her previous finds, and Lucy had somehow imbued him with her enthusiasm for the treasure-awaiting excavation out in the barely-mapped wilds of the Great American Desert, as it was then known: treasure not of gold, but of bones.

Somehow he had agreed to back her bid for a grant to finance an expedition into the little-known area on the borders of Utah and northern Colorado, sparsely populated by settlers and the haunt of outlaws and renegade Indians. *Why?* he wondered, as the boiling maelstrom at the mouth of the gorge loomed up. He must have been mad!

But, suddenly, they hit it, and he could only glimpse the great rock walls on either side as the raft plunged through the swirling waves reverberating from those walls and slid forward over the sucking, spuming water. For minutes that seemed hours there was nothing they could do or think about but, as George Dowson said, hang onto the swirling, spinning, bouncing raft.

'Help!' Lucy screamed.

Matt saw through the spray of water that she had been buffeted from the raft and was overboard. And, then, she was gone. A sense of horror gripped him. But, no! She was tossed up again and being swept alongside. He held onto his stanchion with his right grip and leaned out to grab at her clothing with his left hand and somehow managed to haul her back onto the raft as they went tossing and spinning on through the canyon.

The raftsman's face was grim as he struggled to hold them on course. They were going at such speed even he must have feared they would be smashed to perdition against the rocks and walls. At one point they were slammed into a sucking hellhole of a cul-de-sac, but as Lucy hung on, Matt reached out to pole them off, and they went flying on their way again.

But Lucy screamed as she saw that the buffeting was having even more dire effects. A sharp rock must have cut through the ropes and their precious equipment was slowly, but irrevocably, sliding away to be lost beneath the maw of white water. All those hours they had spent listing what they would need — gone for good!

All that time spent working out how they would get to that area of the Rocky Mountain chain where, she was convinced, the treasure they were seeking might be found! They had travelled in Pullman comfort on the trans-continental railroad from Chicago, across the Mississippi to Omaha, and on across the rolling Western plains through Cheyenne and south Wyoming to Wamsutter, disembarking at the small halt of Rock Springs.

From there, George Dowson had confidently assured them he could transport them and their equipment down the Green River to their destination, the confluence of the Yampa River. So much for his words.

'God's teeth!' Lucy gritted the words out, looking around her as finally the rapids were behind them and they slowed into a calmer bend of the river. 'Everything's gone.'

Matt Strangeways helped pole the raft onto a sandy beach and Lucy scrambled ashore. She had lost her hat, her wet hair clinging to her somewhat bony, if intelligent face, her long travelling dress sodden upon her slim frame.

'Not everything,' he said. 'We're still alive.'

'Mebbe if we hang on here a bit,' their boatman chimed in, 'some of your boxes will be washed along.' He looked a tad guilty as he tied up, hoping they wouldn't blame him for their loss. 'I'll git a fire lit. The young leddy'd better git them clothes dried out.'

'Oh!' Lucy gave a deep sigh of exasperation. Her trunk of spare clothes and personal items had gone, but, more importantly to her, their boxes of canned food and other supplies, flour, sugar, coffee, salt, and their maps, ropes, picks, trowels and excavating equipment. 'What on earth are we

6

going to do now?'

'Well, it seems like we made the wrong decision.' Strangeways spoke in an educated voice, unable to suppress a slight smile at Lucy's indignation. 'Perhaps we should have taken the longer route by horseback.'

'Yes, Matt, please' — she jagged back her lips in an expression of intense irritation — 'don't tell me you told me so. Would you kindly cover your ears a minute? I have a feeling I'm going to start cursing.'

Strangeways looked mildly surprised that such a highbrow woman should even be familiar with the language of muleskinners, and hastily tried to calm her, patting her arm and saying, 'Come now, Lucy, you must get out of these saturated garments. These mountains are chill at night. You must get dry before darkness comes on. Dowson is right.'

'We ain't stranded, folks. We still got the raft. Tomorrow we'll push on for Dutch John. It ain't more than forty miles. No way we'll make it tonight.'

The riverman went off to collect kindling and dry wood to see them through the night. Lucy began to drag off her waterlogged costume until she was down to her bodice and knee-length pantalettes which clung to the curves of her body. 'I'm aware this is not socially acceptable back East,' she said, 'but needs must. I'm sure you must be aware of the basics of female anatomy, Professor, even if you are a confirmed bachelor. So please don't be embarrassed. You needn't avert your eyes.'

A blush rose to the temples of Professor Strangeways and his scalp prickled uncomfortably at her words. He did, indeed, have a strong urge to glance at the sinuous young woman in her state of semi-undress, but mentally chided himself for such low, nay, cheap peeping-Tom emotions.

'I assure you, Miss Luffy' — he took off his suit jacket to wrap around her shoulders — 'I think of you only as a valued colleague.'

'Hm? Thank you, Matt.' She pulled the dry and warm jacket tight around her shoulders as Dowson quickly got a fire started. She produced the professor's wallet from the pocket, tossing it to him. 'Perhaps you had better hang on to this. Or we really will be in a hole.'

'Why? Have you lost all your cash?'

'Yes, it seems like it.'

'Don't worry. I've enough to see us through.'

The raftsman soon built up a big blaze and, with his Bowie, cut thin branches which he stuck in the sand to act as a clothes rail. 'May I?' Strangeways picked up Lucy's sodden costume, shaking it out and arranging it over the sticks. For some reason his blush intensified for he was not used to touching female garments. He squeezed out her black stockings and hung them alongside. 'You really ought to dry out your underclothes,' he mumbled.

'Maybe. But I'm not going to sit here stark naked in front of you two.'

'Heh, heh.' Dowson cackled with mirth. 'We ain't gonna object. We don't want ya to catch your death of cold.'

'That's all right,' Lucy remarked. 'I'll dry my front side first and my backside next. We haven't even got a blanket between us. Gosh, what a state to get into.'

'We better huddle together tonight. You 'tween us two men for warmth.' Dowson gave a wolfish grin. 'Don't worry, missy, I ain't gonna molest ya. I'm a married man. And I'm sure the perfessor ain't.'

Strangeways blush intensified again. 'Of course, I'm sure that is wise.'

'Waal, I still got my rifle.' Dowson jumped to his feet clutching the longarm. 'I'll go see whether I can shoot us some supper. But don't hold out too much hope.'

He had a curious curled ram's horn, capped by a silver lid, on his belt, which he opened. 'Me powder's dry.' With a nail of his finger he prised open a compartment in the Kentucky's butt. 'So are me patches.' He wrapped one around a Minié ball and poked it down the barrel with the muzzle-loader. 'Wish me luck, folks.'

They watched him lope off along the river-bank as the sun began to fall and the shadow of the gorge's high walls spread over them. Strangeways took a break from feeding the fire to sit down beside her. 'I'm beginning to feel like a ship-wrecked mariner,' he said. 'We may not be on a desert island but we're stuck here with an ocean of wilderness around us.'

To a degree it was true. They could not, obviously, go back up the gorge. To the south-east stretched hundreds of miles of barely inhabited stone plateau and snow-capped mountain ranges of Colorado. To the west was the tangle of salt flats and wind-eroded hills of Utah known as The Canyonlands.

'No need to despair, Professor,' Lucy said. 'All we have to do is follow the river. It's a bad, if not ominous start to our expedition. But I'm not planning on giving up. We will re-stock at Dutch John and carry on. I've come too far to stop now.'

'Well, at least I've still got my specs,' Strangeways remarked, taking them from his waistcoat pocket. He examined the wire-rimmed spectacles. 'I would be lost without them. Not that we've anything to read. All the books and papers are in the river.'

'Yes, that *is* a nuisance. We will need to keep careful records and logs. Maybe I could get by for a while without food but I couldn't live without writing materials.' Suddenly an explosion barrelled out from along the gorge and Lucy, inadvertently, jumped, grabbing one hand at the professor's knee. 'What's that?'

'It sounds like Dowson is shooting supper.' Strangeways smiled, and closed his hand over hers. ''You're getting jumpy, Lucy.'

'I'm sorry.' She wriggled her fingers

free. 'It's this place, it's creepy. I feel somehow vulnerable.'

'Well, I explained to you before, I'm an academic, not a wilderness man.' He was young to be such a renowned professor, just forty, who still had a thick brush of dark hair flecked with grey, which, it was said, gave him a distinguished air. 'You promised me there wouldn't be any trouble.'

'Don't worry, Matt, I'll look after you.'

But, as she jokingly made that reply, there was a movement in a clump of willow trees hanging over the river, and the shadowy shapes of men on horse-back appeared, holding still, watching them.

Lucy tensed. 'Oh, Jesus,' she hissed. 'Who's this?'

'Hallo, the camp,' a gruff voice called. 'We're coming in.'

The riders moved slowly out from the trees and they saw there were six of them, led by a squat old man, full-bellied and gone to seed, wearing a worn topcoat and a squashed stovepipe hat. He was grey-bearded, bright gimlet eyes piercing them as he wiped a drip from his whiskey-blossom nose.

'Well, lookee who we got here, boys. Some city dude an' his near-nekked doxy. Ain' we in luck, I do declare? Where'd you two birds git washed up from?'

'I'd ask you to speak civilly.' Strangeways got to his feet, angered by the man's attitude, but not at all liking the look of the guns he and his *compadres* were toting. 'Our armed guides are out hunting and will return soon.'

'You mean guard, doncha? Yeah, we seen him. The way he shoots I doubt he could guard much anything.'

A broad-shouldered, redheaded fellow leaned on his saddle horn and grinned down at them. 'Now ain't she a purty li'l piece of fluff all ready an' waitin' fer us in her undies?'

The four younger men cackled as they sat hunched in their ragged, dusty clothes on their mustangs. One, with a cleft palate and facial disfigurations that indicated congenital syphilis, croaked, 'Bagsie first poke at duh prize.'

'Shut up, Scut,' the older man growled. 'Ain't I taught you to respect womanhood? First things first. You better hand over what valuables you possess, girlie. Rings, bracelets, diamond necklaces.'

'You're out of luck,' Lucy replied. 'I don't go in for such trinkets. And anyway, we've lost everything of value in the gorge. All our luggage went adrift. All the money I had was in my reticule and that's gone. As you can see we are now destitute. That is God's truth.'

'Yeah?' The old man looked her over, surlily, and turned his attention to Strangeways. 'How about you, mister? You gonna give us the same excuse?'

'It's true.' For a moment it crossed the professor's mind to hurl a burning brand at the horsemen and try to escape. But where to? It would be impossible. So, instead, he tried a half-hearted bluff. 'I lost my cash in that river, too. But I should warn you we are on an official government expedition. The rest of our party will be along soon. If you should dare to touch this young lady there will be a hue and cry. You will all be hunted down and hanged. So you villains had best be off and hasten on your way. We will say no more of it.'

'What's that he called us?' A scrawny, bearded man in a battered hat, its brim hanging down around his ears, drew his Remington New Army revolver and thumbed the hammer. 'Villins?'

'Hold it, Fee.' The leader of the bunch, in his squashed Lincoln hat, beamed at them. 'Who said anythang 'bout hurtin' ya? Search him, Red.'

The husky young fellow, his massive shoulders taut beneath a lumberjack shirt, in corduroy pants and heavy boots, leaped down and grabbed Strangeways by the throat. He raised him with a one-handed grip like steel and ran him back to slam up against the bole of a fir. He ran his left hand about his body, frisking him. 'He ain't armed. Hey, what's this?' He dug in the professor's back pocket and produced his wallet, brandishing it as he tossed the man away. 'Looks like we hit the jackpot, Jesse.' The professor tumbled back and hit his head against the trunk of the pine.

'Fer Chris'sakes, how many times I told you not to call me by my name,' the old man shouted. 'Now they'll know who we is. Gimme that.'

Red scowled and tossed it to him. He knelt beside the half-conscious professor, jerked a silver enscrolled watch on its chain from Strangeways' trouser fob pocket, and cried, 'I'm having this!'

'*The Lord giveth and the Lord taketh away.*' Jesse smiled as he counted the greenbacks. 'Whadda ya know! Near on two hundred dollars. He blesseth us this day.'

'Yeah!' Scud hollered, as he jumped from his mount and snatched hold of Lucy. 'An' He's givin' me this bitch today. C'mon, Trick, hold the wild cat down.'

The young woman screamed and fought to get away as the syphilitic's grimy hands clawed at her body through her damp linen underwear, his deformed mouth leering at her, his eyes gleaming as he groped at her breasts and tried to kiss her. Desperately, she scratched at his face and kneed him, viciously, in the groin.

Suddenly Dowson's voice rang out. He was standing there behind them, his Kentucky raised to his shoulder. 'Hold it, you scum. Unhand that young leddy. I'm giving you ten seconds to git on your hosses and git outa here. Or' — he had the rifle pointed at the old man — 'he gits it.'

'Hey, that ain't friendly, neighbour,' Jesse drawled. 'My boys only havin' a bit of fun.'

'Yah.' Scud was doubled up, his hands between his legs. 'We gonna teach this bitch a lesson.'

'You'll do no such thing,' Dowson

ordered. 'Just drop those shootin' irons nice and slowly, then do as I say, ride outa here.'

'Sure, raftsman.' Fee already had his gun in his hand and hauled his horse around in an arc, his arm outstretched, the Remington aimed point blank at the riverman's chest. The bullet ploughed into Dowson, knocking him to the ground as his Kentucky exploded sending its ball whistling past the old man's head. 'Like that, you mean?'

He watched Dowson on the sand, gasping like a landed fish, and grinned, finishing him with a second shot. 'That settled his hash.'

'Whoo! He durn near kilt me,' Jesse growled. 'Thanks, Fee. Come on, boys, we gotta get outa here.'

'What about her?' The taller man, called Trick, had got hold of Lucy from behind, his strong arms wound firmly around her. 'Ain't we — ?'

'I said we're leaving. Put her down,' the old man bellowed. 'You can find yourself another doxy. We ain't got time to wait on you. All this shootin' has let 'em know where we are. C'mon. We're gittin' out *now*.'

'Shall I finish 'em?' the tall man had pulled a knife and pricked it to Lucy's throat, while Strangeways, half-stunned, on the ground, watched helplessly.

'Nah. Leave 'em. They ain't gonna cause us no trouble.' Jesse raised a finger to his hat by way of goodbye. 'You may thank the Lord for smiling on you, too, today, young woman.'

He slashed at his horse with a wrist quirt and went riding along the river away from Flaming Gorge. The others clambered onto their broncs and went charging after him, disappearing into the dusk.

Shamefacedly, Strangeways felt at his man-handled throat and jaw, got to his feet and went to silently comfort the girl, taking her in his arms. 'They've gone,' he said. 'It's all over.'

Lucy allowed herself to sink her head against his shoulder and gave some gasping sobs, before pressing him away.

'I'm all right, Matt. I can cope.'

She went to sit by the fire, half-naked, her bodice torn from her breasts, covering herself with her arms, and gave a shudder. 'Yes, I suppose I should thank the Lord they didn't have their way with me. I'm OK. But look at poor Dowson.'

'He was very brave.' Strangeways went over to stare down at him. 'We'll take his body in to Dutch John tomorrow.'

2

'Well, I know they call it the Wild West but I never in my wildest dreams expected anything like this.' Professor Strangeways gave a deep sigh of desperation and sat before their campfire, his head in his hands. 'That's all our money gone now. What are we going to do? We are hundreds of miles from anywhere. How are we going to survive?'

'Here's your jacket back, Matt. Put it on.' Lucy Luffy had pulled the worn black reefer jacket from Dowson's corpse and draped it around her shoulders. 'This will do for me.'

She picked up the Kentucky rifle and examined it. 'We will survive like others survive by killing our food.' She stuffed the powder horn and bag of shot into the jacket's capacious pockets. 'I should be able to handle this. I'll see Dowson's widow gets paid for it and his full two months' wages. It's the least we can do.'

'Are you crazy? What do we pay her with?'

'We still have funds in Chicago. We will telegraph for a banker's draft to be sent to the nearest bank.'

'Telegraph? How? The last telegraph line I saw was back at the railroad. Where exactly, pray tell me, would this bank be?' He waved an arm south-eastwards across the landscape of grey and desolate hills, the Roan plateau, stretching, indeed, for a hundred miles, rising to the distant jagged peaks of the Rockies, more than 4,000 ft in altitude, which could still be seen through the dusk arrayed in awesome tints of sunset reds and purples. 'Look! Where the devil will we find a bank? All we can do, Lucy, is try to get back to the railroad and call this whole thing off.'

'Cheer up, Matt. No need to sink into the slough of despond. I'm not going back. Maybe we can get help in Dutch John. If the worst comes to the worst we can always raft on down to the town of Green River.'

'Are you mad? Raft on down? Through what godawful other rapids? It's nearly five hundred miles.'

'No, there shouldn't be any more rapids until you reach the Colorado, at least, from what I remember from the map. And there must be a stage-line back from Green River to Grand Junction and on across Colorado Territory to Denver. All isn't lost, Professor. It's not the end of the world.'

'It feels like it,' he said, glumly. 'Why on earth did I ever let you talk me into giving up my nice comfortable office at the museum to come out to these god-forsaken parts on some wild goosechase?'

'It's not a goosechase, Matt. I've done my homework. I'm pretty certain we'll succeed. Think of the plaudits you'll get back in Chicago. I've got very reliable information as to the where-abouts of the site.'

'Just exactly who gave you this information?'

'Two Fogs.'

'Two Fogs?'

'Yes, he's an Indian. A Ute. I met him on my last trip. He showed me a fossil. He knows where we should dig.'

'An Indian? We've come all this way on the say-so of some ignorant savage? Just because he sold you a fossil he happened across?'

'He isn't ignorant. In his way he is very wise. He will lead us there.'

'So, how are you going to contact this Three Fogs?'

'Two Fogs,' Lucy corrected. 'Well, I admit that might be a problem. But he indicated the general location. We should be able to get there without him. Anyway, Matt, I'm going to try. What have we got to lose now?'

'True.' He threw his hands up in a Gallic shrug, raising his eyes heavenwards. 'Oh, God, Lucy, I wish I had your optimism. Your nerve. Where do you get it from?'

'Well,' she replied with a brash smile, 'perhaps we're the superior sex. I've noticed some men can be remarkably spineless.'

'I'm sorry.' Strangeways stared at her with genuine admiration. 'I asked for that. I'm behaving badly. I'll try to be braver for you, Lucy. Let's say more positive. To start with, what are we going to kill to eat? And how will we skin it when we do? How cook it?'

'Ah, yes. We'll be needing Dowson's Bowie and his tin box of matches. I'll start on easier game first, Matt, like jack-rabbits.'

They could still hear the distant thrumming roar of the gorge, but above it suddenly came men's shouts, the whinnying of horses. Lucy grabbed hold of the long arm. 'Who now?' she asked.

Whoever it was approached their fire carefully, jumping from their mustangs and dodging forward through the rocks and pines to surround them. They could see through the moonlit night the top of a hat or raised carbine. 'Throw out your guns and put up your hands,' a man called, 'or we come in shootin'.'

'Wait!' Lucy shouted, getting to her feet and tossing the rifle away. 'Don't shoot. If it's that man Jesse you're after, he's gone.'

There were a few moments of silence while whoever it was chewed on this, then a tall man in a leather topcoat, and flat-crowned hat, remounted and walked his horse slowly forward, a carbine in one hand and pointed their way. 'Show yourselves,' he shouted.

'I can't show you much more,' Lucy muttered, irritably, pulling the reefer jacket tight to cover her torn bodice modestly. 'I'm practically naked.'

Strangeways stood up beside her and shouted, 'They attacked and robbed us. They killed our guide. Who are you?'

'Bounty hunter.' The man was chawing on a wad of baccy in his cheek, and he surveyed them with intense blue eyes from beneath the shadow of his hat. He spat a brown gob of juice on to a rock. 'There's a price on them varmints' heads. Did you say, *Jesse?*

27

Was he an older guy?'

'Yes, and there was some mentally deficient called Scud who tried to have his way with my colleague. Fortunately she fought him off and retained her virtue.'

Lucy smiled, brightly. 'What remains of it.'

Both Strangeways and the horseman gave her odd, quizzical looks. Was she joking or what?

'That'll be Scud Greer. You're lucky to be alive, ma'am, if he had his hands on you. He's Jesse Greer's boy.'

'A thin-faced one, Fee, did the killing,' Strangeways said. 'And what did they call that tall one? A funny name . . . Trick. Then there was a big pug-ugly, Red, who thumped me.'

'We know them. Fee Fisher, a cold-blooded killer and Trick Greer, one of the cousins. Was there another with 'em?'

'Yes, similarly scruffy and mean, a squint to his eye,' Strangeways replied. 'They didn't mention his name. They looked like they'd been in the saddle a long while.'

'Yeah, we been after 'em from way back.' Two other men had silently joined the bounty hunter. 'That'll be that no-account runt Wilk Price. How long ago they gone?'

'Don't know. They took my watch. Only two hours or so, isn't it, Lucy? She's been through a terrible ordeal. I don't suppose you could take us into the nearest town?'

The bounty hunter sat his horse and considered this. 'It would mean we'd have to ride two-up. We were gonna try an' catch up with 'em tonight. No, I guess we'd better help you folks.' He swung down from his horse and offered his hand to Strangeways. 'The handle's Jim Roland. This here's Hank Brown and Chris Meade. What's happened to your gear?'

'We lost it all in the gorge,' Lucy said. 'We're absolutely bereft. If you could get us to a bank, that would be a help.'

'A bank?' Roland gave a downturned

grin. 'There ain't many of them in these parts. I guess, first of all, we better boil up some cawfee and share what grub we got, eh, boys?'

He nodded to the two others who swung down and began to rummage in their saddle-bags. He eyed the half-dressed Lucy with a mixture of curiosity and amused lechery. 'What's a pretty gal like you doin' out here in these parts?'

'The professor and I are on an official expedition, with the full backing of the Department of the Interior and our Chicago museum.'

'The perfessor? You ain't wed, then?'

'No, we are colleagues. Not,' she said, 'that that has anything to do with it.'

Jim Roland leaned his carbine against a rock and uncinched his saddle. 'Maybe we'll catch up with them bozos tomorrow. It's too dark for nightridin'. Too much cloud.' He dumped the saddle and bedroll by the fire, sat down and leaned his back against it. 'So, what exactly, are you lookin' for out here?'

'Dinosaurs.'

'Dinosaurs? There ain't any of them about. If there were I'd have noticed.'

'Not living ones. Dead ones. I'm talking a hundred and forty-three million years ago.' Lucy decided to sit down, too, opposite him. 'We are palaeontologists.'

'Pally — what — ogists?'

'We excavate their bones, hopefully. I am reliably informed their remains might be found in the hills south of here.'

'We are deadly serious,' Strangeways butted in. 'We're leading members of the American Geological Society. Unfortunately we have lost all our equipment and now our cash, too.'

'Waal, whadda ya know?' The bounty hunter cut himself another chaw of tobacco and stuffed it in his cheek. 'Thass bad luck.'

'It certainly is,' Lucy agreed. 'Do you really enjoy that disgusting habit?'

Roland met her eyes, and laconically spat into the fire. 'You mean chawin'? Sure I do. It keeps you alert. Keeps the hunger at bay. You wanna slice?'

'I really find it most disagreeable. On trains, in the streets, even restaurants, everywhere you go, all this expectorating, it's most offensive. However, there we are. I suppose I'm in no position to lecture you.'

'No, maybe you ain't.' Roland idly watched his two companions putting a coffee pot on to boil, unwrapping some dry tack biscuits and jerky. 'That's true. In fact, I'd say it's not exactly polite when we're about to share what we got with you. I was even thinkin' of lendin' you a blanket to cover up them very distractin' and shapely legs of yourn. You didn't oughta be goin' givin' us no ideas.'

'Men!' Lucy shook back her damp hair. 'Is that all you ever think of? However, the loan of a blanket would be appreciated.'

'Yeah, I guess it would.' Roland leaned over, untied his bedroll and tossed a blanket to her. 'Be my guest.'

The jerked meat and biscuits was not

very palatable and tough on the teeth, but it was food, and there was hot black coffee to wash it down. Lucy began to feel warmer and more secure with the three armed men around. To tell the truth being manhandled by the two scruffy ruffians had shaken her up more than she cared to admit. 'Eugh!' She shuddered as she recalled their over-powering stench. 'What horrible men.'

'Is that longarm the only protection you got?' the bounty hunter asked. 'Apart from human predators, aincha worried about grizzlies? My advice would be to arm yourselves with a repeating rifle or a six-shooter.'

'I strongly believe that guns only encourage violence. I've travelled alone on horseback through Indian Territory and parts of Colorado before and have not had any trouble . . . well, apart from once before.'[1]

'Maybe, but you've had a taste of violence today. Out here guns are a

---

[1] See Rogue Railroad.

necessary evil. If you don't like killing you'd better hire somebody better than him' — he jerked his thumb at Dowson's prostrate corpse — 'to protect you.'

'Perhaps you have a point,' she replied, 'but first we have to raise the cash.'

'That ain't gonna be easy,' one of the other men, Meade, muttered. 'Mebbe you oughta go back?'

'No, I'm not doing that,' Lucy said firmly. 'I think my clothes should be dry now.' She stood, holding the blanket around her waist and felt at her caped travelling costume and stockings. 'Yes, lovely and dry. If you gentlemen will excuse me' — she backed away with her bundle of clothes into the darkness of the pines — 'I will try to make myself more presentable.'

Jim Roland raised one eyebrow, mockingly, at Strangeways. 'That's quite a spunky gal you got there, Professor.'

★ ★ ★

Lucy woke in a misty dawn to see the bounty hunter kneeling on the raft checking the knots of the ropes. 'What are you doing?' she called.

'I guess I better come with you to see you safe to Dutch John,' he shouted. 'The boys can take the raftsman's corpse in.'

'That's not necessary,' she told his companion, Hank, as he handed her a tin mug of coffee. 'We will be holding you up.'

'Aw, we'll catch up with them varmints sooner or later.' He grinned at her, amiably. 'There ain't no hurry. The more crimes they commit the more bounty'll be on 'em.'

'Isn't that a rather callous attitude?' Strangeways asked. 'Aren't you concerned about others who might suffer at the hands of those criminals?'

Hank shrugged. 'It ain't nuthin' to do with me. I'd just as soon say so long. But it seems Jim thinks he better see you get to some place safe. He ain't allus been a bounty hunter. So he's got this soft streak. Gonna be his downfall.'

'Really?' Strangeways asked. 'What was he before?'

'Aw, I dunno. It's a long story.'

'Well, even if he is a paid killer,' Lucy remarked, as with her fingers she tried to comb straight her wind-straggled hair, 'it's nice to know he has some sort of social conscience.'

'We ain't killers, ma'am,' Meade put in, gruffly. 'We're administering justice, doing folks a favour by ridding the territory of some of these scumbags. Agreed, it puts cash in our pockets. Let's make a move, shall we?'

★　★　★

It took most of the day to pole the raft along the fast-flowing river. The bounty hunter hardly spoke, just taking his stand at the rear of the raft in his fringed hide coat, hanging onto the rudder pole, his blue eyes alert beneath the brim of his flat-crowned hat, occasionally shouting out an order to

Lucy or Strangeways to watch out for various rocks, or to pole them further away from the bank. They had no further incident and by mid-afternoon, propelled on by the current, they spied a collection of log cabins built on a rise above an inlet.

They poled slowly into a landing stage and the bounty hunter explained, 'There used to be just one trading store owned by Dutch John. He got hisself killed by an Injin. Now it's run by Panos the Greek, but the old name's stuck. As you see there's a few other traders arrived to service what few hunters and ranchers there are around here. It's gettin' to be almost a township. But there ain't no bank nor no telegraph wire.'

'Howdy.' A lean man in a black frock coat and bootlace tie hailed them from the landing stage. In his natty striped trousers tucked into polished boots he looked more like a gambler than what he proclaimed himself to be. 'I'm the sheriff here. Hear tell you folks have had some trouble.'

'You ain't gonna get no help from that jackanapes,' Jim Roland muttered. 'So it's no use you thinkin' you will. Your best bet's go see the Greek.'

Strangeways glanced at him and called out, 'We've been robbed, Sheriff.'

'It was Jesse Greer's gang,' Roland said, spitting a gob of tobacco in the sheriff's direction.

'So I heard. Your boys beat you here by three hours. They're over at the saloon.'

'Yuh, they would be.' The bounty hunter tossed a rope to the sheriff to tie up the raft. 'You gonna help us go after 'em, Greaves?'

Luke Greaves gave a crooked grin from beneath his pencil moustache. 'You know I cain't do that, Jim. I don't git paid enough to go chasin' all over the territory. I'm town sheriff, thassal. You bring the Greers in I'll see they git hanged and you git what's comin' to you.'

'Yeah, and while we do the dirty work

you'll be sat on your idle butt over at the Longhorn.'

Greaves flicked back his greasy hair and offered a hand to Lucy to disembark. 'Doncha listen to him, miss. He knows my duties lie here.'

'But wouldn't your duty be to go after them, Sheriff?'

'Afraid not, miss. What happened to you is way out of my jurisdiction.' A bevy of onlookers, women in long dresses and sunbonnets, weather-beaten farmers, and ragged children, had gathered to watch. 'My duty is to protect this town,' Greaves shouted at them. 'It's all right, the young woman ain't been hurt. You can all get about your business.'

'But are we to get no redress?' Lucy asked, standing on the rickety landing stage. 'No assistance from you? We are destitute.'

'Ain't nuthin' I can do for you, young lady. I don't run no charitable organization. If Roland here brings in the Greers, which I doubt, and if they still got your stolen cash, which I doubt even more, you can have it back. Meanwhile maybe you and your man could get work washin' dishes over at the saloon. That's up to you. What the hell you doin' raftin' through Flaming Gorge for, anyhow?'

'My partner and I are on an expedition.'

'What you exper-ditioning for? Gold? There ain't none of that in the hills around here.' Greaves looked her over and gave a cackling leer. 'Looks like you might have a shapely leg under them skirts. Maybe the Longhorn would take you on as a dancin' gal.'

'Watch your mouth, Sheriff,' Jim Roland butted in. 'This here's an educated lady.'

'Well, I ain't suggestin' she go peddle her butt, am I?' Greaves gave an oily smile, a diamond in one tooth twinkling. 'That's up to her. But there's only one gold mine she's got and that's what she uses to sit on.'

The bounty hunter pressed Lucy aside and grabbed Greaves by his shirt at the throat with his left hand, bunching his right fist to take a punch at him. 'You filthy — '

Lucy caught hold of his arm. 'Leave him,' she cried. 'He doesn't bother me. And I'm sure it must be an offence to strike the law officer.'

Reluctantly, Roland loosened his grip and thrust Greaves away. 'You're asking for it, Greaves. One of these days — '

'Yeah?' the sheriff sneered, straightening his shirt, adjusting the silver longhorn woggle holding his bootlace tie. 'I can't wait to put you in the cooler, pal. But today I'll forget about it. I'm in the middle of a game. You're free to go.' At which, he turned on his heel and sauntered over to a rough-hewn plank hall which bore in crude red lettering the motif: 'Longhorn Saloon, steam beer and whiskey, gambling and darnsin' gals.' He glanced back at them, before adjusting his sidearm and stepping inside.

'That useless sidewinder,' Jim Roland muttered. 'I wouldn't trust him an inch.

He's got this town tied up.'

'Forget him, Mr Roland,' Lucy said. 'Perhaps you'd like to introduce us to Panos the Greek?'

'No, I gotta go find Hank and Meade. We gotta be movin' if we're to catch up with the Greers. It's my guess they'll be miles from here by now.' He tipped a finger to his hat and smiled at the girl, revealing tobacco-stained teeth. 'You can't miss his joint. It's along the way a bit. If anybody'll help you out he will.'

'If not,' she replied, returning his smile, 'if you ever come back this way you might find me kicking up my knees as a dancing girl.'

Strangeways quickly intervened. 'She's joking, Jim. No way that will happen.' He offered his hand to him. 'Thanks for your help, Mr Roland. Don't worry about us. We'll survive.'

'I sure hope so.' The tall bounty hunter turned and ambled away with a loose easy stride, his spurs clinking, towards the saloon. Without looking back he raised a hand in farewell.

3

News of the travellers' plight had reached Panos the Greek. A curly-haired man, running to fat, he stood in his shirt sleeves and apron and watched them approach his trading store. '*Herete!*' he called. 'Welcome! What can I do for you?'

'It's a bit difficult.' Strangeways looked around at the array of shirts, blankets, guns, hats, barrels of dried apples and hickory nuts, sides of bacon, sacks of flour, all mixed up with harness, ropes and shovels in the solid log cabin. To one side were a couple of tables and chairs and an appetizing scent of cooking was drifting from a kitchen at the rear. He shuffled awkwardly, unaccustomed to begging. 'We're in a spot, you see . . .'

'The truth is we need credit,' Lucy butted in. 'A fellow called Roland told us you might arrange a loan. We have funds in Chicago. If you could give us two hundred dollars we'd be glad to pay interest of, say, ten per cent.'

'Thass a lot of money.' Panos chewed on a tooth pick and considered them. 'I got a lot of people wanting credit. Farmers, settlers, strangers passing through. Some of these people can't pay or I never see them again.'

'Well, what can I say?' Lucy spread her hands and met his eyes. 'I can only give you my word.'

'Oh, I dunno. *I* have to think about it.'

Panos Panayotis had emigrated from Crete to New York in search of the promised land. He had toiled for a while in that city as an undercook in the kitchens of Delmonico's and had picked up some hazy ideas of high-class cuisine. But when he had heard that gold had been found in Colorado he and his wife had gone west by railroad and joined the stampede of miners in Denver. Hard work with a shovel and panning in an icy stream had provided a few pokes of dust, enough for a wagon and team, and he had pushed on through the mountain passes following a new stampede to a town called Bonanza only to find dreams of riches again eluded him.

However, when he reached the Green River and headed north he found the stretches of fertile green land between the walls of grey rocky plateau, and the distant snow-capped mountains, reminded him strongly of his homeland. At Dutch John the erstwhile owner of the trading store had just been shot dead in a gambling dispute. He had no known heirs and the place was being auctioned. On the spur of the moment Panos bought the place with his last fifty-dollar poke of dust.

'Business not good,' he mused. 'You see, I have to be careful.'

'What you do?' A woman more rotund than himself, in faded black and a headscarf, emerged from the kitchen and berated him in shrill Greek. 'Where is your hospitality? Can you not see these travellers are in trouble? Have you become so American you forget our Cretan ways?'

She caught hold of Lucy's arm and propelled her to a chair. 'Here, you sit,' she said in English. 'I breeng you coffee. Take no notice of heem. He theenk only of dollar.'

Panos grinned, bashfully. 'Thees is my wife, I breeng her from Greece. She keep me in order. Sure, I geev you loan. Panos trust you. Now, what you want eat, huh? My cooking it rival that of the great Delmonico's. Here is menu. You like?'

He beckoned Strangeways to the table, hastily found glasses for water. With a flourish he presented a pink flower to Lucy. 'For the beautiful lady. You had bad time. You be OK now. Ten per cent too much. Five per cent fine. You pay me when you can.'

'This is very good of you,' Lucy said, as Mrs Panayotis brought in tiny cups of tarry coffee. '*Efcharisto*.'

'You spik Grik?' the black-moustachioed

woman exclaimed.

'Only a little. When I was eighteen I joined my first expedition to the ruins of Olympia.'

This united their friendship and they talked excitedly, Mrs Panayotis insisting they should stay in their back room. 'It's good of you but there is only one bed,' Lucy said when they inspected it. 'You see we are not married.'

'I'll take the floor,' Strangeways offered. 'We can rig a blanket up as a curtain.'

'Not married?' the woman screeched. 'Why not?' She caught hold of the professor's arm. 'She ees lovely lady. Why you no marry her? It only cost two dollar. Why you waste time? We go get preacher. He marry you. Then tonight you both sleep in big bed.'

'No, I'm sorry.' Strangeways raised his hands to quieten her. 'I couldn't possibly marry, not that Miss Luffy would accept me. A wife and children would hamper my routine. I am a bachelor.'

'Pah! Bachelor. Don' you know what you miss?'

'The professor's right,' Lucy put in. 'Ours is a partnership of minds. Our family is our scientific work. And, anyway, I have no time or use for men in the manner you are proposing, Mrs Panayotis. I am too busy.'

'No time? Pah!' The woman registered her disgust. 'You wash. I cook. You eat.' And went bustling away

Lucy shrugged and smiled at the professor. 'That was a narrow squeak. A few more minutes and she would have had us wed. I think she means well.'

Strangeways stared at her as she poured water into a bowl. 'I . . . er . . . meant no disrespect. It would of course be a great honour . . . but . . . '

'That's OK, Matt. We're both bachelors at heart. See, I told you we would be OK. It's rather fun, isn't it?'

After they had washed and tidied themselves they studied the menu. 'What's this?' Strangeways exclaimed. 'Braised foreribs of Cork. Broad Beams.

48

Stuffed Aborigines.'

Lucy tried to restrain a smile. 'I'm afraid Mr Panayotis's spelling of English is about as good as my Greek.'

Strangeways looked puzzled. 'Let's hope they taste better than they sound.'

'I think he means aubergines.' The menu was full of other surprises: 'Chef's liver on toast. Green pee soup. Frilled steak with gritted tomatoes.'

'What you wan', folks?' Panos asked, arriving with a napkin draped over his arm.

'I think I'll have some of your chef's liver.' Lucy giggled. 'Followed by jam fart.'

'Ver' good. You wan' drink? Vino? Ouzo?'

'The professor's teetotal. He doesn't approve.'

'Ah, too bad. Wass matter with heem?' He poked the professor with his fist. 'Don' he like have fun? He real sad sack, huh?'

'The water is fine,' the professor said, primly, rather shocked by Lucy's vulgarity. What next, he wondered, fearfully. Would she get drunk and jump about Greek dancing with this sweaty fat fellow? It wouldn't surprise him. She seemed suddenly to lack inhibitions. Not the serious-minded girl he had imagined her to be.

There was much screeching and caterwauling in the kitchen, but the food when it arrived was surprisingly good, flavoured with mountain herbs. Panos lit the lanterns, and they leaned back in their chairs, talking about the places in the Peloponnese she had visited.

They were so busy laughing and talking, Lucy had not noticed two rough-looking men who had entered the store and were stood watching and listening. One was a muscular man in a woollen hat, corduroy knee britches and boots. The other was an older more shabby individual, with tufty white hair and beard, a jaunty hat and long topcoat revealing the sheen of age.

'Howdy,' the big one said. 'You the

couple who got robbed?'

'That's right,' Strangeways replied. 'They stole two hundred dollars in brand new notes. All I had. Why?'

'Sounds like you need protection.' Big George Larsen scratched at his belly beneath his tartan shirt and beamed at them. 'This is dangerous country. You need bodyguards and guides if you're plannin' on goin' someplace.'

'And you're planning to be them?' Lucy replied. 'What think you, Panos?'

'Big George plenty tough.' The Greek appraised the two men. 'But I not sure about his pal. He look like my goat, old, skinny, and gettin' past it.'

'Doncha worry 'bout me.' The old guy tipped his hat over his eye to an even jauntier angle. 'I kin shoot the eye out of a squirrel.' He drew back his ankle-length overcoat and whipped a big Bowie from his belt. 'If it comes to knives I'll cut the tripes outa any who try it on with us, be it white man or savage.'

'Well I never!' Lucy was taken aback by the blood-curdling language. 'Your references would seem impeccable. I'm almost inclined to believe you. But can you handle horses and hump heavy equipment?'

'Feel that, lady.' The skinny character offered his arm crooked at the elbow to tense his biceps. 'Go on, feel it.'

When Lucy did so, tentatively, she exclaimed, 'My word!'

'There y'are. Hard as a billiard ball, ain't it. Mississippi Fred at your service, lady. You won't have no need to complain about my work.'

'Well, we will certainly be needing a couple of men to set up camp, hunt, and maybe give a hand with the excavating. But, you may have heard, our funds have been severely depleted. We could only offer you two dollars a day.'

'Make it three and we're yours,' Larsen put in, slapping her hand before she could nay-say.

'Just a minute, Lucy.' Matthew

Strangeways caught hold of her arm, and pulled her aside, lowering his voice. 'Don't get carried away by the ouzo glow. How do you know we can trust these two jaybirds?'

'Jailbirds?' Larsen strained to listen but misheard. 'We ain't jailbirds.'

'No, Big George OK.' Panos the Greek patted her shoulder, reassuringly. 'He done work for me. Other one I never set eyes on, but hired hands hard to come by in these parts. Maybe the best offer you get.'

'Right, you're hired.' Lucy shook hands with Larsen, whose grip almost crushed her knuckles. She gave a wincing smile at the other one. 'We'll get organized in the morning.'

'Good!' Panos beamed. 'Now I play bouzouki. You drink. You eat. You dance. OK?'

★   ★   ★

'We're lucky it's a full moon tonight,' Hank Brown called across to his

53

companions as they rode along the bank of the Green River. 'It's fit to rise. We should be able to make up some time on those varmints.'

'Don't tempt fate talking about luck,' Jim Roland replied. 'We ain't had much of it lately.'

He looked up at the huge globe of moon that, indeed, was sliding up out from behind the dark-cut silhouette of crags above their heads which marked the opening of Crazy Woman Creek. His sharp eyes raked the rocks and sand of the river edge. All around was suddenly bathed in silver moonglow. Hoofprints could be clearly seen indicating their prey had entered the narrow ravine. 'Looks like they're gonna head over the hills to Bonanza.'

'It's our bonanza I'm interested in,' Chris Meade called out, 'when we catch up with these sage rats.'

'All right, keep your voices down,' Roland called across to his fellow riders. 'They may have camped higher up the creek.' He sniffed the air, curiously. 'I could swear I can smell the varmints.'

'Well, it ain't likely any of 'em's had a bath since last Christmas, if then.' Hank Brown gave his barrel-chested laugh. 'So that don't mean a lot. You could smell 'em twenty miles away.'

However, after that the three men cut out their chatter and pushed on in silent caution up the gloomy, high-walled creek. The only sound that could be heard was the clatter of their horses' shoes on boulders alongside the stream, the snort of their breath, and the creak of harnesses.

But to Wilk Price, keeping watch from a pinnacle of rock on a bend of Crazy Woman Creek, the sounds were warning enough, jerking him from a half-dozing sleep. He tugged the butt of his Sharps single-shot rifle into his shoulder, fiddling with the sights as the shadowy shapes of the three pursuers came into view down below in the creek. His .50 calibre, favoured by buffalo hunters, could deliver maximum power at maximum range. He grinned, wolfishly, as he took aim at Jim Roland's distinctive grey, the pinhead becoming aligned in the v-notch of the sights. Wilk might have a squint eye, but it was no handicap to his shooting. He took first squeeze on the trigger and whispered, 'Take that, you bastard!'

The first Roland knew of disaster was when his grey mare, Sissy, squealed with pain and fear as lead smashed into her jugular and she went down gouting blood. Her rider's instinctive reaction was to kick his feet out of the bentwood stirrups and try to jump clear before the big horse rolled on him. He leapt away to take cover behind a boulder and heard the clap of the rifle shot from up on the heights barrelling away off the walls of the ravine. He watched the mare screaming and kicking in her death throes until she slumped still. 'Hot damn,' he said. 'That was a fifty-dollar horse.'

'You see anything?' Chris Meade called, as he peered up at the cliff from where the flash of gunshot had come.

'Whoever it is must have a single shot,' Hank muttered. 'If he had a repeater one or two of us might be already dead.'

Jim Roland had crawled forward to take cover behind his dead horse and he reached to pull his Winchester carbine from the scabbard. 'Whoever it is has got us pinned down,' he said, 'but if it's a single shot that gives us a chance to get close.'

No sooner had he spoken than a volley of shooting from the cliff-top sent bullets spitting and ricocheting off rocks about their heads for Wilk had been joined by Jesse and the boys. They had been alerted by Wilk's shot and come running. Or as fast as they could negotiate the climb up the narrow goat-track to the top of the cliff from the ruined log cabin, where they had planned to stay the night.

The corpulent Jesse was the last to arrive, puffing and panting from the exertion. 'Well done, Wilk,' he wheezed. 'It's them damned bounty hunters been tailin' us. Don't they ever give up?'

'Yee-haugh!' Wilk yelled, as he loosed another bullet from his Sharps, which whipped the hat from Hank's head as he ran forward to join Jim Roland. 'Nearly got that fat pig!'

'Nearly ain't good enough,' Red shouted. 'You shoulda gone for the man not the hoss. Now they're well dug in.'

The boys yipped and hollered as they sent lead flying down into the ravine trying to dislodge their pursuers from the cover of the big horse. But all they did was splatter them with blood. The bedlam of shooting, however, sent the other two horses skittering back down the ravine.

When the onslaught of lead slowed, Jim Roland stuck his head up and tried taking a succession of shots at their assailants on the cliff, rapidly levering the 12-shot Winchester, feeding .44 calibre shells into the breech, but he knew it was to little avail. A carbine was no match for the range of a rifle.

He ducked down as more bullets

whistled about him with murderous intent. 'Aw, shee-it!' He gave a long drawn-out whistle between his teeth and cursed some more. 'These boys are costing us time and cash. What's more they're gittin' me mad.'

Up on the cliff, Jesse Greer gave a roaring laugh of satisfaction. 'That'll make 'em think twice about chasin' us. Red, Fee, Trick, you come with me. We're gittin' out. Wilk and Scud, you stay here and keep 'em occupied 'til we're packed-up and gawn. We'll leave your hosses ready saddled.'

'Aw, why me, Pa?' Scud moaned.

'Doncha worry, boy,' Jesse shouted, as he scuttled away. 'We'll wait for you at the head of the crik.'

There was little the three bounty hunters could do. When the shooting on the cliff ceased, they ran forward cautiously, towards the bend in the river only to see Scud and Wilk high-tailing it away on their mustangs. They cracked out shots from their carbines after them but to no effect.

Jim Roland stood tall, his gun smoking. 'What did I tell you? It don't do to talk about your luck,' he muttered, ' 'til the rat's in the bag.'

★ ★ ★

When Roland rode back two-up behind Hank to the small settlement of Dutch John, Chris cantering alongside them, they were greeted by the sound of bouzouki, fiddle and drum. The folks seemed to be having a fine old time in Panos the Greek's place. 'Come on,' Jim said, 'Let's take a look.'

They pushed through a throng of children and rubberneckers peering through the doors and windows at the shenanigans inside. A makeshift band, led by Panos, was pumping out melodies, settlers and traders sitting at tables were clapping in unison to the beat, as the prim and proper Lucy Luffy, in bare feet, her mane of hair fallen down and flailing across her face, went spinning and leaping, her hands held aloft, her fingers snapping, demonstrating the way they danced far away over the ocean in old Crete.

When her eyes met Jim Roland's she ceased, and a smile lit up her face. 'You're back early,' she called. 'Did you catch them?'

'Nah.' Roland scratched his nose in some embarrassment. 'They caught us. They shot my hoss from under me.'

'Good Lord!' Lucy exclaimed, as the music slowed, and she smoothed her hair from her eyes. 'The infallible frontiersman. I am surprised. And sorry, of course, for your horse.'

She walked over to resume her seat at Professor Strangeways' table, the gentleman in question looking decidedly disapproving of her wild behaviour.

'I'm sorry, Matt,' she smiled. 'It's something about that Cretan music gets into me.' She sprawled back on a rickety chair, raised her eyes and puffed upwards at a stray coil of hair. 'I'm bushed.'

'I'd say you were drunk,' the

professor replied, drily.

'Hey, don't be such a dog in the manger,' Roland cut in. 'The young lady's enjoying herself.' He leaned his carbine against the wall, peeled off his leather coat to toss on the floor, and removed his hat to reveal a thick mass of flaxen hair which he pushed away from his eyes. 'How about it, lady?' His icy-blue eyes met hers and he held out his arms. 'Can I have the pleasure?'

Lucy hesitated, examining the rangy man-hunter. 'Well, I told you, you might find me kicking up my knees when you got back. Why not?'

'If you'll excuse me, Professor,' Jim said, with a grin, as he caught hold of one of her dainty hands. Lucy sprang up and began prancing around on the balls of her feet in a most peculiar manner as Panos started strumming again. 'This sure ain't a dance I'm familiar with, but I'm gittin' the hang of it.'

Professor Strangeways watched them, even more disapprovingly. Lucy gave a shrill scream — 'Yassu!' — and spun on tiptoes as Roland kicked and thumped his boots on the floorboards, and yelled, 'Yas-sir!' The two of them were laughing and spinning, their bodies far too close, in a most uncouth and intimate manner, as people stamped and clapped approval. It was not at all to the professor's liking.

The last straw came when the forward Westerner asked, towards the end of the evening, whether she'd like to step outside to take a look at the full moon, and Lucy giggled, hung onto his arm, and disappeared with him. It was too much for Strangeways. The calamitous end to a truly dreadful two days. It was time to retire to bed.

'Goodnight, Matt,' Lucy called, when she finally returned to their room a good half-hour later. 'What a lovely day it's been. I told you everything would turn out for the best.'

Strangeways did not reply, but lay and listened to her rustling, her snatches of song, and splashing as she brushed her teeth behind their make-shift curtain, and her girlish giggle before she finally succumbed to the embrace of sleep. His body was hard and tense, unable to relax, his heart thumping with jealous anger. Goodness gracious, he chided himself, silently. Why on earth did I ever come? This is a disaster. What on earth is wrong with me? If only I had a book to read. What have I got myself into? If only I could get back to civilization. I must have been mad. I'm beginning to think *she* is mad, too. She is not the girl I thought I knew.

4

'Three cartons of wax candles, six bars of soap, a hatchet, an adze, three shovels, two clasp knives, flour, sugar, rice, raisins, a jar of oil, a tin of salt and a dozen cans of Blue Hen tomatoes.' Miss Luffy was a different, more serious-faced lady in the morning as she stood in Panos's store ticking off her list of provisions. 'Oh, and a sack of pinto beans.'

The Greek had given her an old accounts book and a handful of pencils, the best he could offer in stationery for it wasn't much in demand in those parts. 'I'll take six pairs of these summer hose, two of these wool shirts for working in.'

'Blankets, rope, frying-pan, tin mugs and bowl, spoons, forks, water canteens,' Panos sang out, adding to the pile. 'Don't forget flints, matches, shot and powder for that old rifle of the riverman.'

'Ah, yes, I must see to his burial, poor Dowson. Is there an undertaker's in town?'

'Thass me.' Panos beamed at her. 'For two dollars I dig grave and say few words from Bible. You gonna need tarpaulin panniers to carry all your stuff. We go buy you some pack-horses now. Panos get fair price for you.'

'Hadn't we better see to Mr Dowson first? I must send some cash to his widow, too. Gosh, my head, I shouldn't have imbibed so much last night. There's so much to do.'

'Don't you worry. We soon get you fixed up. You be ready to hit the road by noon.'

'Good. You're a treasure, Panos.' Lucy hesitated before saying, 'I wonder, have you seen Jim . . . Mr Roland?'

'Sure, I see him head out first light. Him and the other two.'

'Ah, right, I thought maybe he could give me some advice on the best route.'

'Don't worry. I take wagon into Bonanza for supplies. I show you way.'

'Is there a bank in Bonanza?'

'Sure. But the gold seam all run out now. Thass why everyone moved on. Some miners keep digging but all they make is a few dollars paydirt a day.'

Professor Strangeways emerged from their bedroom, tying his loose tie, washed and shaven. 'Good morning,' he said. 'What's going on?'

'I'm restocking.' Lucy forced a smile of greeting. 'These paint-scrapers should be fine for use in the dig, and some paint brushes, too, for the finds.'

'*If* we find any,' Strangeways remarked, dolefully.

'We will. We don't want any doubters on this expedition, Matt. Maybe you could find those two men we took on and see to loading up the pack horses Panos is going to purchase for us?'

'Whass hurry?' the storekeeper asked. 'First you have breakfast, ham and eggs. How you like? Sunny side up?'

'No.' Lucy made a wry grimace. 'Not

67

for me. I couldn't face it. Just black coffee.'

After they had breakfasted, Panos's wife fussing about them, trying to force Lucy to eat, the Greek loaded up Dowson's body, stitched in a canvas bag, on his wagon and drove out along the river someway to a patch where there were some mounds of graves and rough-hewn crosses at their heads. He jumped down, began digging vigorously and, when he was hip-deep, told them to haul the corpse in. When the riverman was buried and well tamped down Panos recited some Greek from his Bible, crossed himself, and sprinkled ouzo from a bottle over him.

'A drink for the dead,' he said, with a grin, taking a swig himself.

Lucy declined the offer of one herself, with a downturned jag of her lips, and knelt to offer a prayer for his soul.

'Tragedy has struck early.' She regained her feet and glanced at them. 'Let's hope we have no more trouble.'

'I'm not so sure about that,' Strange-ways muttered. 'I've got a funny feeling in my insides . . . '

'You're just homesick, Matt. Just think, this is a once-in-a-lifetime chance to make our name. The sun is shining; life is wonderful. Look at the river, the mountains. We have a month or more of summer left and I intend to make the most of every minute of it. If you really want to go back say so now, Matt. You can go into Bonanza with Panos and ride on south from there. But, if you stay I want to hear no more of your doubts.'

'How can I leave you?' Strangeways sighed. 'I would never forgive myself. I'm sorry, I guess I've got into a bit of a foolish funk. I'll try to put on a brave face from here on.'

'Good.' Lucy smiled and squeezed his hands. 'Come on. We've a lot to do.'

As she strode away, Strangeways lowered his voice and nudged the Greek. 'Do you think you could provide me with a decent revolver?'

'Sure, I got a nice li'l storekeeper, four-inch barrel, Colt .36. It fit nice an' snug in your pocket. I put it on bill and pack two boxes bullets, OK? You make sure you protect the lady. You a lucky man to have her.'

★   ★   ★

When they finally got under way, they had a mule and two runty nags carrying their baggage and Lucy was confident they were well-prepared for a month's sojourn in the mountains. Big George in his woollen hat and check lumber jacket had taken the lead and Mississippi Fred brought up the rear, each in charge of a pack horse, while Miss Luffy herself had the bad-tempered mule on a leading rein. Strangeways, an inexperienced rider, had enough to do just staying in the saddle.

Panos was trundling his four-horse wagon along the rocky riverside, cracking his whip, and occasionally shouting out items of information. When they turned into Crazy Woman Creek and passed the deserted cabin, Lucy asked who it had belonged to.

'A po-faced prospector called Elmer Longstreet,' Panos replied, morosely. 'A hard, miserable man. He rarely come into Dutch John. His wife go crazy, scratching herself, tearing hair, shouting bad words at people. She go striding about, real loco. Longstreet was sure he would strike gold here, but he never did. One day he brought wife's corpse in, said he found her hanging from tree. Maybe she hang herself. Maybe he hang her. Who knows? After that Elmer disappear.'

Lucy gave an involuntary shudder. 'What a mournful story.'

'It was the cabin fever,' Big George put in. 'Cooped up in there all through the winter snows. It ain't good to be too alone.'

'Come on,' Panos shouted. 'We got a stiff climb ahead. We need to get to Connor's Crag 'fore nightfall. Yee-haugh!' He slapped his reins over the horses' backs and went rumbling and bouncing away along the high-walled canyon.

Bonanza had been 'one helluva town' in its day, a whooping, howling, live-it-up boom town, to which panhandlers, miners, gamblers and goodtime girls flocked, tents and shanties soon making way for a main street of ramshackle stores, billiard parlours, boarding-houses, hotels, cathouses, and some splendid saloons where men spent their day's dust with abandon and the roulette wheels never ceased turning, night or day.

Now Bonanza was a shadow of its former self, like a decrepit old whore, still painted and hopeful, but neglected and finding it hard to make a dime. Its numerous saloons were generally deserted. Its hillsides were pitted with played-out mine shafts. Some diehards still hung on, dusty desert rats, living in their shacks and scraping the last of the ore from the ground. There was still life in Bonanza, but it was the ghost of the former self.

When Jesse Greer and his boys rode in, they hitched their horses outside the Palace of Varieties, its paint-peeling curlicued false front still announcing its attractions: 'Can Can girls', 'artistes of world renown', 'nightly music hall', 'spiritous liquors, Kansas steam beers', and 'the biggest and best-stocked bar in the West'. Sure, the roulette tales were still there, but the wheels were no longer turning. There was the sign of the tiger over the faro game, but it was no longer surrounded by miners yelling and eager to gamble away their silver.

The thirty-foot-long mahogany bar, specially imported from Denver, with its mirrored back-bar, still stood proud but there was only one barkeep now plying a desultory trade. A big chandelier was suspended from the ceiling but nobody bothered to light its candles these days. And below it, on a torn horsehair sofa that had long since seen better days, were the last of the dancing girls: three ladies of uncertain age but not virtue, their faces greasily painted to hide the marks of dissolution and decay, in tawdry lace dresses and stained shantung, yawning and swatting at flies as they contemplated what would seem to be yet another unprofitable day.

The whores' attention sharpened as Jesse Greer, in his concertinaed top hat and dusty topcoat, swaggered in and ordered in a loud voice, 'Redeye. The best in the house.'

The young bartender jumped from his stool to serve them. 'A bottle?'

'No, you dimwit,' Jesse roared. 'One for each of us.'

The scrawny Fee, the lanky Trick, the squint-eyed Wilk, the syphilitic Scud and the broad-shouldered Red gathered about him and snatched at the bottles, jerking out the corks and spitting them away, before tipping the searing liquor down their throats.

'Jeez,' Wilk sighed. 'That cuts the dust.'

He leaned back against the bar on his elbows and took a gander at the girls who were trying to arrange their limbs and stained apparel in a more appealing manner and simpering like a trio of doves. Soiled doves, they were generally called.

'Who's he looking at?' Wandering Hands Wanda asked, hoicking up her copious breasts to give the dusty stranger a better view. 'Me or you?'

'Me, of course,' her skinny sister-in-sin, Red Hot Ruby, as she was known, replied. 'Who would want a fat, sweaty cow like you?'

'You're both mistaken,' Helga, the ice-cool Swede, drawled, as she lay back and kicked out her black-stockinged legs. 'He's got one eye on me and the other on the door.'

'Hey, darlin',' Ruby called. 'You got a drink to spare for a thirsty girl?'

'Thirsty and naughty, too,' Wanda giggled, as Wilk grinned gap-teeth, and clomped over towards them in his heavy boots.

'Howdy, ma'am,' he said. 'I like what I see. Would them goodies of yours be for sale to a hungry man?'

Now none of them were sure who the heavily squinting Wilk was looking at, but all took the initiative, reaching out clawing hands to grab hold of his various parts, like three spiders dragging their prey into their hole.

'Hey, steady on,' Wilk protested, as he was pulled sprawling across them. 'Ye're spilling my juice.'

'Look at them three hellcats, Pa,' Scud whooped. 'Their hands are gittin' everywhere on poor ole Wilk.'

'He don't seem to be protesting too hard!' Jesse beamed across at the bevy of past-their-prime beauties. 'Go git your share, boys. Me, I'm happy here with my potion. This is real fine ratjuice, mister. I've only bitten into half the bottle and I'm gittin' all fired-up inside.'

'That's five dollars a bottle, the finest Kentucky bourbon.' The 'keep adjusted his celluloid collar and totted up the bill. 'Six bottles, makes thirty dollars, sir. The gals are two dollars apiece, tipping optional, but generally expected for extras depending on what goes on. Clean and honest girls, sir, I might add.'

'They better be.' Jesse showed his little yellow teeth and scratched at his scraggy beard. 'I don't want my boy Scud catching no cupid's measles. Ooh!' He clapped his hand to his mouth. 'I shouldn't have said that.' He was referring to the fact that he had revealed Scud's name. 'Now you're going to know who we are.'

The barman eyed him somewhat apprehensively. 'Would you like to settle now, sir, thirty-six dollars?'

'You jokin', sonny? What's the matter?' Jesse Greer adjusted the long-barrelled revolver in his belt. 'Don't you trust us?'

'I . . . er . . . it's company policy.'

'You jest go about your business, boy. I decide when to pay. You'll be gittin' what's comin' to you, don't you worry.'

The 'boys' had clambered up a wide staircase with the 'girls' and tumbled them into a couple of bedrooms opening on to a balcony from which now emanated a hullabaloo of Johnny Reb yells and yahoos mingled with shrill feminine screams. Wandering Hands Wanda tumbled out of one of the rooms followed by Scud who grabbed her by the hair and dragged her into the next-door room. 'Come on, Red,' he hollered. 'I done with this un. You takin' your time, aincha, Wilk? Gimme a go with your skinny hoo-er.'

After a deal of fighting and shouting, he lurched from the room with his arm around Swedish Helga, the only one of the ladies who appeared to be enjoying the all-in wrestling, took a quick sup from the bottle and shoved her into the first room to join Trick and Fee.

Jesse Greer smirked at the 'keep, who was polishing glasses. 'My boy Scud's a terror for the wimmin. A chip off the old block. I showed 'em a trick or two in my day.'

The young barman glanced up nervously at the activities on the balcony. 'I'd be obliged if you'd ask your boys to show a bit more respect. Wanda and me are engaged to be wed. We're just waitin' 'til we got enough saved.'

Jesse gave a roar of laughter. 'You don't say? What's a pint-size like you gonna do with a big gal like her? You'll look like a dung fly on the backside of a mare.'

Another crash and shrill scream from one of the rooms made the 'keep grip the bar top, his knuckles whitening. 'They're acting awful rough.'

'Sure, it'll be good for her. Only way to treat a woman. She'll know now who's boss.' Jesse frowned at the boy. 'Don't you do nuthin' foolish now. What you got by way of vittles? The boys are goin' to be hungry after this.'

'I can fix you steaks, twenty cents apiece. Fresh beef.' He anxiously kept his eyes on the upstairs rooms as he replied. 'Or there's a sheep's head stew.'

'Make it three streaks each. We gotta keep up our strength.' The bourbon was taking its effect, making Jesse maudlin, his voice slurred. 'What's your name, son?'

'Henry . . . Henry Love.'

'Well, listen, my little Love. Just to show I mean you well I'm gonna settle up our bill.' Jesse pulled Strangeways' $200 from his topcoat pocket. 'You see, I'm a wealthy man. How much do we owe?'

'Let's see, thirty-six dollars plus three dollars sixty cents for the food. You want fried onions?'

'Sure, all the trimmings.' Jesse peeled off the new greenbacks. 'There's forty, keep the change. Have a nice wedding.'

'Thank you, sir.'

'By the way, Henry, you got a lawman in Bonanza?'

'Yessir, we got a part-time sheriff, Dan Hagerty.' Henry glanced up at a big wall clock. It showed two in the afternoon. 'But he's probably locked up and having his siesta by now.'

'Good,' Jesse growled. 'We won't bother him, will we?'

'No, sir.' Henry glanced even more apprehensively at Greer and up at the balcony where Scud had staggered out, his arm around Helga, and was singing raucously, waving the whiskey bottle. 'I'll go tell the cook.'

Some while later, when Jesse and the boys had filled their bellies, and the doxies were still sprawled in a daze up in their rooms feeling like they'd been run over by a stampede, the tubby patriarch called out to Henry Love, 'Say, when's the bank close?'

'Four o'clock, sir,' Henry replied politely, as he brought a tray of beers to wash the steaks down.

'Good,' Jesse beamed, picking at his teeth with a fingernail. 'I'm gettin' a bit low on funds. Need to make a withdrawal.'

'What exactly is your business, Mr er . . . ?' Love ventured, as he passed the foaming glasses around.

'You gittin' kinda nosy, aincha, son?' Greer replied, gruffly. 'As a matter of fact I deal in property.'

'Yeah,' Scud grinned. 'Stolen property.'

'Shut up, boy, with your foolin'. You go out see to the hosses, be ready to leave. Pleasant as it's been we have to be moving on.'

Jesse winked at the other desperadoes sprawled around their table. 'You ready, boys? Drink up. We got business to attend to.' He staggered, drunkenly, to his feet, pulled his Buntline Special revolver, with its fourteen-inch barrel, from his belt, spun the cylinder, putting it to his ear, and stuffed it back again. 'Here,' he said, tossing another five dollar bill to Love. 'Thass for you and the gals. Nobody says us Missouri boys don't pay our way.'

He led his gang, in their dusty topcoats and broadbrimmed hats, swaggering out of the Palace, calling, 'So long, y'all,' and paused in the shade of the sidewalk, casing the sunny street. But all appeared to be quiet. Scud was already trying to tighten the cinches of their horses and gathering the reins in readiness. 'Let's go,' Jesse growled.

He crossed the street, followed by the others, to the once splendid brick-built bank, and pushed through the big oak doors. Red and Trick stayed outside, taking a stand, fists gripping their holstered sidearms, ready to draw.

Jesse accustomed his eyes to the bank's shady interior, annoyed to see a middle-aged sodbuster at the only open grille, arguing with the clerk about credit. Jesse clumped across, caught the man's shoulder and thrust him aside. 'Outa my way, short-arse. I'm in a hurry.'

Fee and Wilk pulled rifles from the cover of their coats as Jesse thrust his long revolver through the bars of the grille and poked it into the bank clerk's face. 'Just gimme everythang you got, son, if you wanna see another sunrise.'

The bald-headed cashier gave a startled squawk and called in a tremolo, 'Mr Roberts, you better come quick. We got trouble.'

Roberts, the bank manager, in a frock

coat and cravat, appeared from his office. 'What is it?'

'This gentleman wants everything we got, sir.'

'Oh, yes?' The manager rubbed his hands and stroked back his greasy hair, eyes darting, as if wondering whether to make a dash for the back door. 'I see. Well, we don't have a lot. These are not prosperous times. Give him what you have in the till, Meldrun.'

'An' the rest you got in the safe,' Jesse replied. 'Open up an' let me through or he gits it.'

Roberts took a deep breath and reluctantly let the whiskey-breath Greer through, leading him to his office and unlocking his safe. 'See, that's all there is.' He began handing out wads of bills for Jesse to stuff into his pockets. 'No more than three hundred dollars.'

'Oh, yeah?' Jesse hoicked him up by his cravat and raised the revolver as if to bludgeon him. 'Where's the rest, you little town rat?'

'That's all, I swear. You can have the

coin and those few pokes of gold dust. Things are bad in Bonanza. We're thinking of shutting up shop. I suppose we'll have to now if you're cleaning us out.'

'Yeah.' Greer scowled and tossed him away, snatching his ruby tie pin, too. 'You won't be needing this. Ouch!' He yelled as the pin stuck in his thumb. Suddenly the whiskey haze hit him and, as he fumbled for whatever else he could find in the safe, he dropped the Buntline, which exploded, the bullet smashing into his left boot. 'Aagh!' He began hopping about cursing vociferously. 'Now look what you done.'

Apart from the scalding pain, his mind was in a whirl, as if the bourbon was slopping his brain from side to side and he couldn't stand up straight. The manager took advantage of Greer's distress to back away into his office and fumble, frantically, in his desk drawer. 'Ah!' He braced himself, slipping the safety catch from his Allen and Hopkins' little ivory-handled .32. He returned to the main room and aimed at the bandit's broad back.

'Oops!' At that moment Jesse Greer lost his balance and crashed back to sit in a wastepaper basket. 'What 'n hell?' Why had the stupid banker, he wondered, shot his own clerk, what was his name, Meldrun, in the back?

'What in tarnation's goin' on?' Wilk shouted as the little bald cashier collapsed to the floor and began caterwauling worse than Jesse had. 'Drop that peashooter, mister.'

Banker Roberts had no intention of so doing. His blood was up and he aimed the .32 at Wilk Price. Whether his hand was shaking too much from fear or excitement, or what . . . the bullet ricocheted off a bar of the counter grille and whined plunging into the chest of the old farmer, who had his hands in the air.

'You kilt the carrot picker, you dang fool.' Before the banker could go for a third shot Wilk fired his Sharps rifle from the hip and sent him tumbling into oblivion. 'There, that settles his hash.'

'Help me up!' Jesse was roaring, for his backside was firmly wedged in the waste basket. When Fee did so, Jesse fumbled to retrieve his fallen Buntline and in the process banged his head on the bank counter. 'Aw, jeez,' he moaned, 'it's one of those days.'

'Come on,' Fee cried, helping him to hop out of the bank. 'Where's the broncs?'

But Scud was having difficulty with the half-wild mustangs, and was way down the street trying to hang on to six sets of reins of the bucking and kicking beasts.

Now that Jesse was out, Red and Trick started off to help with the horses, but the shooting had aroused the town. A butcher came from a shop and blasted his hog-slaughtering gun at Trick, who cartwheeled like a potted rabbit and lay prone in the dust. Red turned and his Navy Colt took out the butcher, who tumbled back into a tub of blood and guts.

However, when Red swung on to his mustang and set off back along the street his saddle began to slowly slip around — the drunken Scud had failed to tighten the cinch enough — and before he knew it Red was hanging upside down before kicking his boots from the saddle and hitting the dust hard. 'Hot damn!' he yelled in disgust, as he sat up, legs outstretched. 'Can't that idjit do anythang right?'

Meanwhile, as Jesse hopped along towards the horses, the front window of the Palace of Varieties was smashed and Henry Love poked a rifle through the broken glass. 'They've robbed the bank!' he screamed and began blamming away at the outlaws.

Wilk swung his Sharps around to reply but suddenly realized he had spent his one shot and had forgotten in the confusion to reload. 'Shee'it!' He dived behind a horse trough for cover.

Fee, trying to drag the hopping Jesse along, saw that their ill-gotten gains were tumbling from the pocket they had been hastily stuffed into. He bent to try to retrieve them, with the result that the fat old man tripped over him.

'Aw, fer Chris'sakes,' Fee yelled, as he watched the greenbacks go fluttering away on the breeze down the main street. 'We're losing it all.'

But there was no time for idle chatter because other townsfolk had begun crashing out bullets, joining in the battle, and lead was whining and carooming everywhere. Fee had to draw his revolver and reply as best he could from a kneeling position.

By now Wilk, behind the trough, had jammed another slug into the spout of his Sharps and took a careful aim at Henry Love. 'Urgh!' the bar-boy gurgled as he felt a pain like a boulder crashing into his chest and, looking down, saw blood gouting out in an arc. 'I'm hit, Wanda dear,' were his last words, as he tumbled out of the window on to the sidewalk.

Wilk reloaded and ran across to kneel

beside the dead 'keep. 'You durn fool,' he admonished, as he snatched the professor's crisp greenbacks from his apron pocket. 'Why you have to butt in, you li'l punk? We was real nice to you.'

Scud had finally got the horses under control and giggled as he clambered aboard one. But his face fell as he looked along and saw his father, Jesse, laying flat out, spread-eagled on his back. 'Aw, no. Pa's day-ed!'

'He ain't dead,' Fee shouted, amid the din of exploding firearms. 'He's damn well snoring. He's pig drunk.'

'Here.' Wilk had retrieved his own mustang, jammed his Sharps in the boot, and loosened his lariat. 'Hold up his boots.'

When Fee did so Wilk flicked the noose over Jesse's feet and jerked it tight, taking a turn around his saddle horn. 'We'll have to friggin' drag him out.'

They finally got into the saddles of their spinning and stomping mustangs and weaved away along the street, shooting their six-guns drunkenly at all and sundry, but, fortunately, thanks to the whiskey, their aim was wild and no one else went down.

In his office, Sheriff Dan Hagerty had been roused from a pleasant dream — about to win a big card game — when he was rudely awakened by the sounds of shooting. 'By thunder, what's going on out there?' he cried, rolling off the cell bunk and searching for his revolver. 'Can't a man get any peace?'

He opened his office door in time to see four riders and two free horses galloping wildly down the main drag towards him in their dust cloud. He cracked out a pot shot, but missed, and his jaw dropped to see a big-bellied man bouncing along behind them attached to a rope. 'What in tarnation? Am I still dreaming?'

As the sheriff spoke and ran out to stare after them, Red turned in the saddle and spent his last bullet, aiming carelessly at the man with the tin star. More by luck than judgement, his slug hammered into the sheriff's belly, making him double up with a groan of despair.

'Oh, no!' Hagerty felt warm blood seep through his fingers as he clutched at his abdomen. He watched the outlaws go pounding along the street and out of town. 'I'm dying,' he moaned, as he expired. 'I knew I should never have taken this job.'

5

When Jim Roland cantered into town on his new twenty-dollar paint horse, Rajah, they were about to bury the dead; banker Roberts, barkeep Love, Sheriff Hagerty, the sodbuster, Mr Williams, butcher George Barton and the lanky outlaw Trick Greer. Bonanza was buzzing with shock. There hadn't been such a shoot-out since its hey-day.

'Let's take a look at the robber's mug,' Jim said.

When the canvas sack was slit open, for nobody had been willing to cough up for a pine box, Trick's face was revealed, snarlingly fixated in death.

'That razor-backed mongrel,' Hank drawled, 'one of the Greer clan. He ain't no great loss to nobody.'

'No, 'cept us,' Chris Meade remarked. 'There was two hundred dollars ree-ward on him.'

'It's no use to the butcher. He's got no kin.' The bank clerk, Meldrun was there, his arm in a sling. 'That ought to be paid to me for all the stress I've been through.'

'If you don't like gittin' shot you better go back East, sonny,' Hank said. 'Banking ain't a safe occupation in these parts.'

'You could take up the question of compensation with the Wyoming governor,' Roland put in. 'He's the one offering the bounty. Jesse Greer and his gang are wanted for a string of offences up north, rustling, stage-robbery, rape, homicide, attempted forgery, horse-theft. Maybe I'd better get in touch with the Colorado judiciary, see if they'd like to top up the price on their heads. OK, you can sew him back up.'

It had been a long two-day ride from Dutch John across the plateau to Bonanza in its ravine, so Jim Roland told his men to go get some eats in the Palace of Varieties and he would join them after he'd sent a telegraph to the

US Marshal's office in Denver. He did so to inform him that the Greer gang were on the rampage in Western Colorado, robbing and killing, and suggesting he should post a reward for their apprehension alive or dead. He signed it, 'a concerned citizen'. The marshal wouldn't take kindly to a bounty hunter twisting his arm. He sent a second cable to the *Rocky Mountain News* office in Denver describing the deaths in brief detail. If they ran a banner headline story that might stir up the judiciary to top-up the Wyoming rewards.

'If Jesse Greer's injured that should slow him up,' he said, when he joined Hank and Chris who were digging into a meal of pork chops, turnips and corn bread. 'We got to get this sorted fast 'fore they send some nosy federal marshals out here to try their luck. We don't need *them* cramping our style.'

Wandering Hands Wanda hip-rolled over to stand beside them, wafting an aroma of cheap perfume. 'You boys fancy a good time?'

'Beat it, sister,' Hank spluttered, through a mouthful of turnips. 'We're busy. Whew! You stink like a Turkish brothel. Move on, will ya? You're puttin' me off my food.'

'You didn't oughta talk to me that way,' the obese and odoriferous Wanda pouted. 'My sweetheart was a hero.'

'Where's the barkeep'?' Jim asked.

'That was him, my hero. We ain't had time to find a replacement,' Wanda said. 'You better go out back and see the cook.'

'Will do.' Roland ambled away, his spurs clinking, but, seeing a bottle of bourbon on the shelf went behind the bar and helped himself.

'Here y'are, boys,' he said, returning with the bottle and three glasses. 'Just what the doctor ordered.' He poured them each a good shot and raised his tumbler. 'Here's to Elijah!'

'Who's he?' Hank asked.

'The Reverend Elijah Craig, of Bourbon County, Kentucky. He invented bourbon in 1789, did the world a great service.'

He savoured the brew and smacked his lips. 'That's more like it. An improvement on the usual coffin varnish.'

'How do you know all these things, Jim?' Chris asked.

'I got a lot of useless knowledge in my head. It ain't ever done me a lot of good. So, where do you figure they've lit out for?'

'Could be any place,' Hank said, pushing his plate away and picking up his glass.

'There ain't many places around if you mean towns,' Jim replied, testily. 'You think they'd try to cross the plateau to Grand Junction? That's more than a hundred miles as the crow flies, but damned hard going if you ain't got wings.'

'No,' Hank mused. 'Or, maybe. You never know. They could be heading east for Denver. But, more likely, they'll turn west, cross back over the line into Utah, try to lose us in the Canyon-lands.'

'God forbid,' Chris exclaimed. 'We'd never find 'em in that maze. Of course, they could be planning to go south along the outlaw trail to New Mexico. On into Texas, or even Old Mexico.'

'Don't say that,' Jim groaned, taking another sup of the bourbon. 'We're fast running out of cash, ourselves.'

'Maybe we better rob a bank?' Hank grinned, and wiped his mouth with his hand. 'No, if I was in their shoes, and I didn't want to go deep south, I'd circle back, cross the Green, and make for Salt Lake City. There's plenty of banks there. The Mormons take care of their cash. They need it with all them wives.'

'Perhaps you've got a point,' Jim said. 'Jesse Greer's as crafty as a sack of snakes. We ain't had no rain in weeks, the ground's as hard as rock. If we don't pick up their spoor soon we'll circle back like Hank suggests. Meanwhile, what's on the menu?'

★   ★   ★

Lucy Luffy, Professor Strangeways and their two teamsters had said so-long to Panos the Greek at the top of Crazy Woman Creek as he ambled on his way to Bonanza. They themselves circled back to the north-west climbing up on to a remote, high plateau to which as yet the maps had given no name but most folks called Bald Mountain.

'It's up here somewhere,' Lucy said, as she tugged on her leading rein at the reluctant mule.

'Yes.' Strangeways, tired and saddle sore, tried to force a patient smile, as he surveyed the vast folds of the bald plateau. 'But *where*, Lucy?'

The young woman called a halt for a coffee-break. 'In fact, I think we'll camp here.'

'We got three more hours of daylight left,' Big George reminded her.

'Yes, I'm aware of that. Would you and your friend be dears and go over to that knot of pines, chop as much firewood as you can, plus plenty of greenstuff.'

'Green needles?' George sounded perplexed. 'You planning on building a bivouac?'

'No, you'll see. Just do as I say, OK?'

She watched the two men stride away, axes over their shoulders. 'I'm going to send a message to Two Fogs.'

Matthew had slid down from his horse to terra firma with a sigh of relief, but raised his eyes to the blue heavens in disbelief. 'Just what are you talking about?'

'I'll show you. Let's get a good fire going.'

When the men returned, laden with branches, she piled the dead ones on her fire and covered them with green ones so that a great cloud of smoke began to billow. 'Don't worry,' she called, 'I'll use my own blanket. If you could hold the other side, Matt.'

'I don't believe it!' The professor coughed as he choked on the smoke. 'Do you really think you can send a smoke signal?'

Big George guffawed. 'She's as crazy

as a loon at full moon.'

'It's simple, really. Similar to our morse code. Now, what did Two Fogs tell me? Two short ones. Come on, Matt, look sharp. Bring over your end. Now take it back again. We'll repeat that. Yes, look, it's working. Now, quick, hold the blanket over while I count to twenty. Right?'

'I'm afraid I've singed my end.'

'Never mind. There it goes.' She stared up, wide-eyed, at the dense puffs of smoke rising into the air. 'That's not too bad, is it? They'll see that from miles away. Come on, we'll try again. We're getting the hang of it now.'

'Well, I never thought . . . ' the professor began, but changed tack. 'Are you sure whoever answers this is going to be friendly?'

Lucy smiled brightly at him. 'We can only hope so.'

Mississippi Fred tipped his hat over his nose and scratched the back of his head as he watched. 'I wouldn't be too sure of that, missy. I heard talk of them

Ute warriors going on the warpath again.'

'Are you trying to frighten us?' Strangeways asked, hastily dropping the blanket.

'Nope, I'm jest tellin' you what I heard. I was along at the White River agency. Nathan Meeker, the agent, he's been trying to force them to be farmers. They don't like it, no, suh, not one li'l bit. Them Ute bucks is turnin' real ugly. There could be trouble.'

'No,' Lucy said, 'I'm sure that's just hearsay. The Utes have been at peace for ages, for thirty years or so. Two Fogs told me so. Then they ceded their lands in '68 in return for a reservation of sixteen million acres. Why should they want war?'

'I've jest told you, Missy, iffen you'll listen. That high and mighty Meeker's the cause. He'd git up anybody's nose.'

'Yeah, I think you'd better stop what you're doing,' Big George growled. 'Nobody with any sense would invite any of them heathen savages up here.'

'Don't be silly.' Lucy looked somewhat dismayed, her smouldering blanket in her hands, but Mississippi Fred had already started dragging the greenery from the fire and was tossing it away. 'You're imagining this, I'm sure.'

'You want to lose your hair, that's up to you,' Big George said. 'But we ain't keen to.'

* * *

'Yee-ikes!' Fee Fisher scrambled out of his soogans as if he'd been bitten, which he nearly had. He grabbed hold of a stout branch amid the kindling of their campfire and poked it into his tarpaulin-covered blanket sack. A rattler slithered out, jaws open, fangs ready to strike. Fee jabbed at it with the stick, hooked it up and hurled it out into the darkness. 'Goddamn! It nearly got me!'

Scud Greer, his ill-shaped gums grinning in a leer, was trying to stifle his giggles. He gave Wilk Price a nudge with his elbow. 'He don't know it was me put dat in dere.'

'What?' Fisher howled, and smacked the branch full into Scud's face, tumbling him off the log he was sitting on. He jumped upon him and began beating him. 'You dang fool brainless barn owl. You ever try that again . . . '

'Oah-aagh!' Jesse Greer gave a long moan and studied the bloody stub of his right toe. 'Quit that racket, will you? I'm in agony here.'

'Piss on it,' Wilk Price drawled.

'What?' Jesse roared. 'What'd you say?'

'Piss on it. It's an old Injin custom. Ain't you heard?'

'What happened to that last bottle of whiskey?' Jesse demanded. 'Have you got it?'

'Yeah, I got it.' Wilk pulled the bottle from his saddle-bag as he leaned his back against the trunk of the fallen tree. 'But I ain't wasting it on your dang foot.'

Jesse watched, his little bloodshot eyes burning like coals in his grey-bearded face. 'Wilk, I need it.

Whiskey'll kill the germs. You ever had a bad tooth pounding its agony into you? This is ten hundred times worse. You don't want me to lose my foot, do you, Wilk? You don't want me to be a cripple for life?'

Price uncorked the bottle, put it to his thin lips and took a long series of swallows, his Adam's apple jerking in his scrawny throat. He gave a gasp and recorked the bottle. 'You think I give a damn about your poxy foot?'

'Please, Wilk.' Jesse extended his hand, pleading for the bottle. 'Don't be like this. Who's in charge of this outfit? Who's been like a father to you, led you outa trouble, kept you safe?'

Wilk shrugged and tossed the bottle to Red, who pushed out his robust chest, taking a deep breath, before taking a long swallow. He pushed the cork back in with his thumb. 'Good stuff. Too good to waste, Jesse.'

Greer gave a roar of anger and pain, snarling like a tree'd puma, as he reached for his Buntline. 'I'll teach you.'

But Wilk had his Springfield across his knees and aimed at him. 'You ain't in a fit state to teach nobody.'

Jesse stared at him, and then at Red, who had loosed the old cap 'n' ball percussion pistol in the scabbard on his belt. 'You ungrateful swine.'

A scream of pain from the bushes, as Scud scrambled on top of Fee and stuck his fingers up his nostrils, diverted the old man. 'Shut up,' he roared.

Red smiled and tossed the bottle back to Wilk, who took another bite. When he held up the bottle the fiery contents were all but gone. 'Too bad,' he said, 'this is our last drop.'

'I'll get you.' Jesse pointed a finger at them across the flickering camp-fire. 'When I've found a quack an' got fixed up. Nobody crosses a Quantrill man.'

There was another cry of pain as the other two scrambled about in the scrub, this time from Scud. Fee had thrown him off and kicked him in the jaw. 'Scud!' Jesse bellowed. 'Come here, you half-wit. Quit your foolin', boy.'

'Quantrill man,' Wilk jeered. 'I'm sick of hearin' about you an' Cole Younger an' Jesse James an' Bloody Bill Anderson. You was just one of four hundred. I bet they didn't give a fat oaf like you the time of day.'

'We were comrades in arms, fightin' for the noble cause,' Jesse moaned, clutching his grimy foot. 'That's somethang you'll never know.'

'It's true.' Scud had appeared, his hair tousled, shirt torn, face bloody, beside the fire. 'Pa was with 'em in the raid on Lawrence. True, ain't it, Pa? You lined them bluebellies up two together an' shot two with one bullet, didn'cha?'

'We had to, boy, to save on ammo.'

'Yeah, and murdered half the civilian population, too, so I heard. Noble cause,' Wilk scoffed. 'You were just a bunch of thieving outlaws lining your own pockets.'

'Kill him, Pa. He can't say that to you,' Scud wailed. 'You were fightin' for the Bonny Blue flag, weren't'cha, Pa?'

'The Black Flag, more like,' Wilk sneered. 'You were just a bunch of pirates, let's face it, Jesse.'

'Ignore him, son. He know not what he says. Come here and piss on my toe.'

'Sure, Pa.' Scud giggled. 'If thass what you want me to do.'

'Good boy,' Jesse beamed, as his son unbuttoned and began to urinate. 'Take a better aim, boy, you gittin it on my pants. What you done to Fee?'

Scud giggled again. 'I think I kilt him. His head's all bloody.'

At that moment Fee appeared out of the darkness, reared up over him, the branch raised in his hands. He gave a mighty swipe. There was a clop like an empty coconut as he connected with Scud's skull. Scud's eyes swivelled before he toppled slowly forward on to the old man, out cold. Jesse collapsed backwards with a shout of anger and pain.

'There that showed him.' Fee grinned, as Wilk passed him the bottle. 'Gee, thanks, Wilk. Just what I need.'

'So, what we gonna do?' Wilk asked Red.

'Jesse says circle back on our tracks towards Dutch John.'

'You figure we still gotta take orders from that old fool?' Wilk asked, his eyes narrowing as he fingered his rifle.

'Sure,' Fee said, going to help the old man up. 'Jesse's the boss. He allus has been.'

'That's right,' Red agreed. 'He's allus looked after us. We ain't gonna kick him in the teeth now jest 'cause the silly fool shot hisself in his own foot.'

'That's right, Red,' Jesse muttered, as he regained his seat. 'Well said. You put that in your pipe, Wilk Price. You ain't takin' over this mob 'til I'm in my box.'

'That might be sooner than you think.' Wilk tipped his hat over his eyes and lay back, the rifle cradled in his arms. 'Good night, boys.'

Jesse wrapped a filthy rag around the blood and bone of his sheared toe, and growled, 'Yeah, git some shut-eye, lads. We got a early start in the mornin'.'

Fee laughed. 'Look's like Scud's already gittin' his.'

6

Sharp, shrill cries came from the band of Ute warriors as they rode their ponies back and forth about the log cabins of the White River agency. A man in a Quaker hat and black, frock-coated suit, stepped from the agency door and fired a shotgun at the Utes. A lance hurled by Two Fogs thudded into his chest and knocked him on to his back. The Uncompahgre chief leapt from his horse, pulled his scalping knife, stood over Nathan Meeker and took his hair. He brandished the bloody trophy and gave a shriek of triumph. 'War!'

Another warrior galloped his mount in close, a bow in his hands drawn back taut. He released the arrow which hissed with unerring aim through the air to embed in the throat of another white man, who was watching from a doorway. Seven more men manning the agency store were dragged out and summarily dispatched by the vengeful Utes, who began looting the store and setting the cabins alight.

'Come,' Two Fogs shouted. 'We will take refuge on Bald Mountain.'

Before they had gone far Two Fogs halted his pony as he saw smoke rising in puffs of clouds from the side of the bare, grey mountain. 'Wait!' he cried. 'These are not Utes. Who can it be trying to talk to us?'

'It is probably a white man's trick,' one of his companions grunted out.

'If so, they will not trick us for long. We will cut their hearts out.' Two Fogs raised his lance. 'Fifteen Lightnings and Rain-in-the-Face will come with me to take a look. You others go on to the cave and wait for us there. If we do not return by nightfall, come to look for us.'

★ ★ ★

111

Big George and Mississippi Fred were snoring rhythmically, rolled in their blankets on the mountainside as dawn rose and Miss Luffy secretively stoked their fire, piled on greenery and tried sending another message to Two Fogs.

'What are you doing, Lucy?' Professor Strangeways looked across from the uncomfortable ledge where he had spent the night, shivering in the morning cold. 'They said — '

'Oh, they're two old women.' Lucy flapped her blanket some more over the thick smoke. 'I don't take orders from them.'·

Mississippi Fred awoke, pushing back his fedora and scratching at his spiky white hair. 'Hey, George, she's at it again.'

Big George stumbled to his feet, anger surging through him. He pulled a green bough from her hands and smacked her a stinging, open-handed blow across her face. 'What did I tell you, you stupid bitch?'

Lucy stumbled back, holding her

stinging cheek. 'How dare you attack me, you oaf? I employ you.'

'Not much longer, you don't.' Big George jerked his Marlin 'Never Miss' revolver from the pocket of his lumberjacket. 'Git over there an' join your pal, sister. Go on, rustle your bustle.'

'What?' Lucy stared at him, indignantly, but when he raised his arm as if to club her with the handgun, she quickly moved over to stand beside the professor. 'What's the matter with you, man?'

'Look, steady on,' Strangeways said, sitting up. 'That's no way to talk to a lady. We won't make any more smoke, will we, Lucy?'

'You sure won't, buster,' George said, holding out his free hand. 'Come on, ante up the rest of them dollars Panos forwarded you. I know you got it. You only spent fifty on the horses and gear. So you must have a hundred and fifty left.'

'You won't get away with this,' Lucy

put in. 'You're not having our money.'

'Just shut your mouth, sister, and you might stay alive. Don't tempt me.' He cocked the 'Never Miss' .41 rimfire at her. 'These never miss. So give.'

'Hold on.' Strangeways leaned over and began feeling in his carpet-bag of belongings, as if for the cash, but his fingers closed over the grip of his 'storekeeper'. Could he, he wondered, take this fellow? 'Where did I put my wallet?'

'Hurry it up,' George ordered. 'We're gittin' outa here. You can take your own chances.'

Mississippi Fred had been watching and got to his feet, opening his long black coat with its worn verdigris sheen of age. He slid out his big Bowie, honed to the sharpness of a razor. 'It ain' no use leavin' witnesses, George. Dead men tell no tales. Dead wimmin neither. We can say the Injins did it.'

'Keep away!' Lucy screamed as Mississippi Fred dived in at her and grabbed her by the hair.

'I'll scalp her,' Fred shouted as he tightened his grip, tugging her towards him and raised the knife. As he did so there was a whistling sound through the air and an arrow thudded into his back.

Big George turned to gape at his stricken comrade as he cried out his pain and shock. Matthew Strangeways took his chance, pulling the snub-nosed .36 calibre 'storekeeper' from his bag, thumbing the hammer and firing into George Larsen's fleshy side. It was his turn to scream, clutching at a bloody hole in his abdomen and tumbling to the ground. Strangeways cocked the pistol again, as gunsmoke drifted, as shocked himself by what he had done, but turning to peer fearfully around at the rocky terrain. There was no sign or sound of the attackers.

'I'm gittin' out.' In spite of the arrow stuck in the back of his shoulder, Mississippi Fred ran to haul himself onto his horse, whipped it around, and went cantering away from the direction the arrow had come. He circled around the rocks and made a dash back down the mountainside, hanging low, slashing his mustang with his wrist quirt, going hell for leather, as they say, terrified of losing his scalp, leaping the mount ploughing down a cliffside of shale, risking it breaking a leg in the descent, reaching the foot of the canyon and racing on back towards Dutch John.

Two Fogs had shown himself, his lance raised ready to throw, watching the white-haired white man go, his long coat-tails flapping. He turned back to face the professor, who had his revolver aimed to fire. Rain-in-the-Face and Fifteen Lightnings raised themselves beside him, fearless, the arrows in their bows drawn back until the strings quivered, ready to let fly.

Lucy stood erect, feeling at her torn hair, staring at the Indians. 'Don't fire!' she hissed at Matt. 'Put the gun down or they'll kill you.'

When Strangeways did so, she called out, 'We are friends. Come forward. We want to speak to you. Two Fogs, don't you remember me?'

'Miss Luffy — is that you?'

'Yes. Don't worry, Matt. They are friends.'

Strangeways remembered certain extremely unpleasant tortures Indians had been known to inflict on their foes and muttered, 'I certainly hope so.'

Two Fogs stepped cautiously forward to join them. He was garbed in a buckskin jacket, decorated and fringed, a store shirt, with fringed leggings and moccasins. There was a single eagle's feather in his long black hair, which was unplaited, and four silver rings in the cartilage of each ear. He was only Lucy's height, and his dark eyes stared at her as he asked, 'What you do here?'

'You said you would show me the cave, Two Fogs.'

'It no good now. You should go. There been trouble. Bad trouble.' He pointed his lance at Strangeways. 'Who he? I kill him for you?'

'No, he is my friend.'

'Who he?' Two Fogs pointed the

lance at George, tumbled in a foetal position, his lifeblood oozing into the dust.

'They were both bad men. They were just about to kill and rob us. Thank you for saving our lives.'

'I owe you a life,' Two Fogs replied. 'You save my son's life.'

Lucy nodded, remembering how she had nursed the boy through his fever, using basic medical skills. 'How is Painted Bird?'

'He is OK. But I tell you it is not good you stay. I kill Agent Meeker. Fifteen Lightnings here kill his store man. Other white men die, too. They bad people. They push us too far. We take no more. It is war between us. The bluecoats come. There will be bad trouble. That is why we come to the mountains.'

'Oh, gosh, Two Fogs, I'm sorry.' Lucy reached out, her face full of concern, and touched his shoulder. 'Why must there always be trouble?'

'Because of the greed of white man,

that is why there is trouble. We offer hand of friendship, but they cheat, and lie and insult us. Now they will hunt us like animals. But many will die. We will not surrender.'

His companions had come forward, garbed similarly to Two Fogs, wearing no warpaint or wampun, just solid, strong, mountain people. They poked at George's corpse and took what little he had of value, most interested in his guns, ammunition and knives. 'Haieh!' Two Fogs called them, touching Miss Luffy's shoulder, brandishing his lance at her. 'This my friend. Good lady. Not many whites good. She good. We not hurt her.'

The two Ute warriors extended their hands to touch hers, nodding their heads, affably. 'Now,' Two Fogs said, 'you must go back to your people. Otherwise I not able to protect you.'

'Oh, please,' Lucy gripped his hand, beseechingly, almost like a child begging a favour. 'You solemnly promised me. We will not interfere in your war.

But we have come all this way. We cannot go back now.'

Suddenly Two Fogs' solemn face broke into a smile. 'You strange lady. OK, I show you. You get killed it not my fault.'

'Thank you,' she cried, 'thank you . . . thank you. Come on, Matt, what are you standing there for? Get the horses loaded. We're moving out.'

Two hours later, after a stiff climb up the mountainside, Two Fogs led them to not so much a cave but a huge overhang of cliff, pointing into the shallow depression. 'There! See! That what I find.'

Lucy, in her long travelling costume, stepped carefully down. 'Where? Oh, my goodness!' She stared at a huge claw print in the rock. 'I can hardly believe my eyes. What can it be?'

Matt had climbed down eagerly to join her. He too, looked stunned. 'It's big enough to be a diplodocus.'

'Perhaps . . . perhaps, who knows.' Lucy looked up at the three Indians. 'May I ask, do you mind if we dig here, possibly take some of our finds back to' — she almost said civilization, but corrected herself — 'to show to people? All the world must hear about this. Two Fogs, I will credit you with the find.'

This time the Ute chief did not smile. 'This bad place. Our legends speak of big animals' — he spread his hands up towards the sky — 'that roam earth before we come. You dig, maybe you let spirits of monsters out to attack us.'

'No,' Lucy smiled, 'I give you my promise these animals are dead. They have been dead for millions of years. They will not rise again.'

'OK.' Two Fogs shrugged. 'You do what you wish. This place haunted. My people will not come here. You good friend. We go to kill bad white people.'

They watched the three warriors go riding off on their horses back down the mountainside until they were lost from sight.

'Matt!' Lucy exclaimed. 'What did I tell you. My heart's thumping with excitement. I can't wait to get started.'

'What about that man I killed? Hadn't I better ride back and report it to the authorities? That other one the Indians got might cause trouble. It bothers me, Lucy. I've never killed a man before.'

'Oh, that! Don't bother about it. How can he harm us? They were just nobodies. Would-be robbers and murderers. You did what you had to do. You acted bravely, Matt.' She frowned and put her finger to her lips, considering. 'Now, I wonder, where should we start? Can you get the scraping tools and marking pegs, Matt?'

'Hadn't we better make camp and get some food inside us first? At least a cup of coffee?'

'Yes, yes, you do that,' she replied, abstractedly. 'I haven't got time. We must make a start before darkness falls.'

* * *

By the time Panos Panoyotis reached Bonanza it had quietened down after the robbery and six killings and was back to its usual sleepy state. But the bank was closed, firmly barred and bolted, a notice scrawled on cardboard: 'Gone outa business.'

'What shall I do?' the swarthy Panoyotis ruminated, scratching his unshaven jaw. 'I got this I.O.U. from Miss Luffy and she needs more funds forwarded from Chicago.'

As the four wagon horses were busy munching the oats in their nosebags, he answered himself. 'I guess we better go on to Grand Junction. It's a hard, one-hundred-mile trail over the plateau. You better be ready to start early in the mornin', girls.'

At least, he would be able to check if his supplies from New York had arrived for he had run out of his most important import, ouzo. 'Doing favours for people always end being bloody nuisance,' he complained, as three miners clamoured around him asking if he would take their pokes of gold dust into the exchange at Grand Junction. 'If

I do I take my ten-per-cent cut,' he said. 'I do business American way from now on. I see you in week or so's time.'

★ ★ ★

Mississippi Fred went charging into Dutch John as if the devil himself was on his tail. He slithered from his sweat-streaming mustang and lurched into the Longhorn saloon, collapsing across the bar. 'Injins!' he croaked out in a hoarse voice. 'They got me. Gimme a whiskey.'

'He's got an arrow in his back!' One of the resident *filles de joie*, Slickfingers Sal, screamed as she pointed at him. 'We're under attack. The savages will slaughter us all.'

The sheriff, Luke Greaves, was enjoying his usual occupation, skinning a settler of his hard-gotten gains in a game of poker. By some change of luck his adversary, a sodbuster called Jed Grimes, had hit a winning streak. With an emergency apparently on his hands up at the bar — a man with an arrow in his back and that stupid doxy, Sal, screaming at the top of her lungpower — he needed to bring the game to a rapid conclusion. Greaves pulled back the skirts of his frockcoat to loosen the silver-engraved Smith & Wesson .44 holstered over the side of his left thigh, butt forward. He favoured the cross-over draw. He jerked his black Stetson over his brow and glanced craftily along at his sidekick, Harry Gilligan, who was leaning back in his chair ten paces away, a shotgun over his knees.

The lanky sheriff got to his feet, reached over and snatched up the carrot-picker's poker hand, slapping it down with disgust. 'Two aces. Where you get them from, you sidewindin' cheat?'

'Take that back. I don't cheat nobody.' Grimes flushed red in the face with indignation, but there was fear in his eyes as he scraped his chair back. 'I play an honest game. Come on, Sheriff, you know that.'

'That's a damnable lie. Come on, draw, you coward.'

There was no alternative for Jed Grimes but to go for the ten-dollar Thunderer stuck in his belt. Before he could hoist it out, however, Luke Greaves had his S & W in his hand. The revolver belched flame and lead blasted the sodbuster's life to extinction.

'I cain't abide card-cheatery,' Luke Greaves drawled, blowing down the barrel of his revolver and returning it to his polished leather holster as the company, stunned into silence by the explosion, turned to see what was happening. 'You all saw what happened. He drew on me. A fair fight, pure and simple.'

The sheriff hitched tight the long-horn toggle of his bootlace tie, running a finger along his pencil moustache in a conceited manner, as he met the silent accusation in the onlookers' eyes. 'Well I'm right, ain't I? Who says different?' As none ventured a reply he scooped in the pot, tipped the coins into his palm, and gave a brief wink at Shotgun Harry. He hadn't needed his help on this occasion but he'd get his cut.

'Now,' Greaves said, clomping across the pineboard floor to the bar. 'What's the cat's chorus about? Calm yourself, Sally.'

'He's got an arrow in him,' she quavered, still pointing.

'Well, pull it out, and somebody go git the quack. Meanwhile, pull that stiff outa here 'fore he stinks up the place.'

Mississippi Fred was gurgling into his whiskey. 'It ain't just the Utes,' he stammered. 'It's them two, them Easterners we took out into the hills. That hoity-toit fancypants, what's her name, Luffy. She's a friend of Two Fogs. She's stirring up the Utes. I shouldn't be surprised if she's behind the uprising. She's 'coon crazy. And he's as bad. He shot my pal, Big George Larsen, in the back, shot and kilt him before my very eyes. Cold-blooded murder if ever I seen it. I pulled myself on a hoss and got out of it. I was lucky to get away with my scalp.'

'Come on, my friend, have another,' the sheriff advised, tipping the bottle to his lips. 'Then you'd better lie down and take it easy 'til the sawbones gits here. I want you alive for the trial.'

'What's going on, Sheriff?' Shotgun Harry asked, his twelve gauge tucked under his brawny arm.

'What's going on? I'll tell you what's going on. Treason. That's what's going on. I never liked the look of them two. I figure they could be spies, come all this way to stir up the Utes to rebellion, to foment trouble and undermine our American way of life.'

'That's terrible,' a woman shrieked. 'I never liked the look of that stuck-up Eastern bitch, neither. The way she was dancing about at Panos's store, showing her legs, depraved and disgusting it was, I swear.'

'She's a friend of Two Fogs. She told us so,' Mississippi Fred coughed out, as he was laid on the floor. 'She sent smoke signals to him. We tried to stop her, but there she was at it again when I woke up. I shouldn't be surprised if she was behind the Meeker massacre. The next we knew there was Two Fogs and his boys peppering us with arrows, and that so-called professor helped them, turned his gun on George' — he gave a strangulated sob — 'gunned down my best pal.'

'Hanging's too good for 'em,' Slickfingers Sal shrieked. 'You gotta do something about this, Sheriff, 'fore they murder us all.'

'Calm down, will you?' Luke Greaves raised his hands to quiet the apparent consternation in the crowd which was getting angrier by the minute as others pushed into the saloon and heard the news. 'Me and Shotgun will ride out this minute and arrest those two. We ain't scared of the Utes, but if any you men want to come along we'll be glad of your help. If so go git yourself horses and guns and meet me outside.'

Several men volunteered and rushed to do as the sheriff suggested. 'I'll go get my own bronc and a rifle,' Luke Greaves announced. 'No need for concern, folks. We'll arrest those two snakes and bring 'em back for a trial, then we'll hang 'em. I don't care if she *is* a woman. It's our lives at stake here.'

'No need to bring 'em back, Sheriff. String 'em up,' a hard-faced settler woman shouted. 'She's a damn witch in my opinion. People like that don't deserve to live.'

'Yeah,' Luke remarked, in a lowered voice to Shotgun Harry, as they made a passage through the hubbub of people. 'I wonder what they really went up into the hills for. Do you think it was gold they were after? We may be on to a good thing here, Gilligan.'

'I never liked the look of that city dude,' Shotgun Harry replied. 'Strangeways is his name and strange ways he undoubtedly has.'

7

Lucy Luffy shovelled earth into a sieve, lifted it to shake, and sifted through for any more bones. It was hard work and by mid-morning her shoulders already ached. She undid a cameo brooch pin at her throat and undid her blouse a few buttons to let what little breeze there was riffle down between her breasts. The sun was baking down from a clear blue sky and a trickle of perspiration ran from beneath her large felt hat down her temple. The summer temperature in these desert regions often soared above 100° Fahrenheit. 'Ah!' she exclaimed with joy, picking out something similar in shape to a plate of false dentures. 'Look, Matt,' she cried. 'What do you think this is?'

Strangeways stepped carefully through their piles of finds across to her as she dusted the 'denture' on her baggy brown skirt and showed it to him. 'Lucy, I believe this is the jawbone of a baby dinosaur.'

'Exactly my idea but I didn't dare say so.' She stared at the little jawbone with wonder. 'God's toenails! Isn't this exciting?'

'Don't let's get carried away. This is all supposition.'

'Come on, Matt, admit it: you're as excited as I am. This is a bigger find than the California tar lake, than the Ozark caves. This area is absolutely crammed with bones.'

'Yes,' he muttered, reaching for the accounts book and licking his pencil tip to note the discovery. 'It's going to be like a giant jigsaw puzzle fitting them all together. We need to proceed with great caution. We will have to sack them up into separate lots for transportation.'

Lucy slipped the little jawbone into her skirt pocket for safety. It was somehow special to her, something the modern world had never seen before. 'It's truly amazing,' she whispered, as she knelt back to her task, using a paint brush to dust away dirt, seeking small bones to add to the skeleton. But, instead, she began to unearth a larger bone, which went on and on and on. 'Holy Jesus,' she cried. 'What's this?'

'Careful,' Matt cautioned, but betrayed his own excitement by grabbing a trowel and digging feverishly away to help her clear the top part of what appeared to be a huge skull. 'Am I dreaming?' he asked, as he paused for breath. 'Tell me I'm not, Lucy.'

'You're not dreaming, Matt.' Lucy had managed to dig down round the side of the skull. 'This is a whole head, teeth as well, probably the mother of that little thing. Matt, we've found it! It can only be a brontosaurus.'

'It's gigantic,' he said, in a hushed voice. 'How are we going to lift it and transport it?'

'I doubt if we would be even able to get it into a railroad goods van.' Lucy stood and stared along the overhang, waving her hand. 'Full grown it would have been as tall as a house and seventy feet long. Is it too much to hope the whole skeleton's entombed in the cliffside?'

'Who knows. This is a treasure trove. What are we going to do with it? This head is too precious to leave here. And no use to anybody out in this desert.'

'So, we'll take it back to Chicago, that's what we'll do.' Lucy reached for a wooden canteen and took a drink of stale, lukewarm water. 'For the first time I miss not having those two bozos, Big George and Fred around. We need someone to help with the heavy lifting, the fetching and carrying.'

'Indeed.' Matt accepted the canteen from her. In this heat the human engine needed plenty of water to keep it going. They were running low and the nearest stream was some miles off. 'They did have their uses.' He gave an involuntary shudder as he remembered the blood pouring out of Big George after he had blasted the bullet into him. So much blood. It was something that would

134

haunt him, he knew. There could well be trouble from it. 'How I wish I'd shot him in the leg, simply disabled him. But the other one had his knife out and was going for you.'

Lucy reached over and squeezed his hand, her eyes concerned for him. 'Don't blame yourself, Matt. It was a split-second decision. After all, they started it.'

'What's that?' he asked, startled by the sound of shooting, rumbling up towards them from down the mountainside.

Lucy climbed in her button-up bootees through the rocks and rubble and out of the defile, peering back the way they had come. It was wild desert country, a vast area of canyons, sagebrush, yucca and juniper. Sporadic sounds of shooting echoed through the hills, seeming to come from a mile or two away, and she thought she could see gunsmoke drifting.

'It must be a hunting party,' she said, returning to him. 'Come on, let's keep digging. We've got a hell of a lot to do.'

★ ★ ★

The Uncompahgres were a resilient mountain people, once part of the powerful Ute empire, who roamed the western fastnesses of Colorado and were renowned for their building of stone forts which they turned into almost invincible strongholds. Since killing Nathan Meeker and riding out from their White River reservation, Two Fogs and his warriors had decided that for the time being until a treaty was agreed they must return to defensive mountain warfare.

Thus it was that the armed posse riding out eagerly from Dutch John to search for Strangeways and Lucy Luffy ran straight into an ambush before they reached Bald Mountain. Two Fogs and his men had seen the spiral of dust kicked up by their horses from five miles away, and had plenty of time to secrete themselves along a steepsided canyon.

A tattoo of arrows drumming into

the ground around them was the first warning the settlers had that they were under attack. One of their men was soon dead with an arrow piercing his throat, going in the front and out the other side, another had caught one in his thigh, and a horse was kicking and struggling, coughing blood, a lance embedded in his chest.

'Take cover,' Sheriff Greaves screamed as the Utes in their hideyholes also peppered the party with lead from their ancient trade rifles. 'Get in behind the rocks.'

From then on it was a matter of swapping bullet for bullet and watching out that an arrow sailing through the sky didn't get you. Soon the battle reached stalemate, a desultory exchange under the hot sun as both sides began to ration their lead.

'It ain't no use,' Shotgun Harry sighed, his weapon unsuitable for such warfare. 'They got us pinned down. We ain't gonna git nowhere today.'

'It ain't our job to fight Utes,' Greaves said. 'That's what the army gits paid for. We'll pull out, take our dead and injured, go back to town, try again tomorrow. This band will probably have moved on by then.'

The chastened posse ambled back to Dutch John, which they reached after nightfall. Most of them headed for the Longhorn saloon where some Dutch courage in the form of Knock 'Em Dead whiskey soon had them bragging about how many Utes they would kill on the 'morrow and debating who had potted the warrior who tumbled from the cliff. He had been found to have Riverman Dowson's musket in his hands.

'That bitch spy musta traded it to them,' Sheriff Greaves drawled. 'They're the sort who cause all this trouble.'

★   ★   ★

Meanwhile the exhausted Lucy and Matt had given up work for the day, and sat on their eyrie with backs to the sunwarmed rock watching the great ball of glowing red sun's protracted descent behind the peaks of the Rockies, marvelling at the crimson and purple colorations of the canyons and plateaux illumined by its flickering rays.

'Colorado is certainly well-named,' Lucy said, as she sipped at a tin cup of scalding black coffee. 'Can you imagine how this land must have looked when these great creatures roamed here? Their very footsteps must have shaken the ground.'

'In those days it would have been damp and covered in ferns and vegetation for them to graze on. Changing climatic conditions must have killed them off,' Matt remarked. 'Well, Lucy, we've certainly got our work cut out. It could take years, nay, decades, to catalogue all these finds.'

A movement in the rocks alerted Lucy, but it was a colour lizard, as it was locally known, scuttling for its hole. It paused, its bright orange head up, tongue flickering, peering at them, most of the weight of its green body carried on its strong back legs. 'That's what the diplodocus would look like magnified many hundreds of times,' Lucy murmured. 'Millions of years before the coming of man.'

'It makes one feel somewhat puny against such a timescale, doesn't it?'

'Perhaps, but it also fills me with a sense of wonder. I want others to know. Matt, we *must* get some of these bones back. Aren't you glad you came?'

The professor smiled, and stroked back his brush of hair; instead of his office pallor, his face was now suntanned, his shirt open at the throat; his suit streaked with red dust; his boots unpolished. 'You're right.' He crooked his arms about her shoulders and gave her a squeeze, staring significantly at her. 'But the best part has been being with you. You're very beautiful, Lucy.'

'Oh, come on, Matt.' Lucy gently shrugged him off, and rose to tend to the fire. 'It's the sunset making you sentimental. Please, don't go getting silly ideas about me. I think it's best we just remain good colleagues.'

Strangeways bit his lip, frowning, trying not to reveal his hurt. 'Perhaps you're right,' he murmured.

★　★　★

Meanwhile, unbeknown to Lucy and Strangeways, a column of 250 US troopers had arrived from Wyoming to deal with the uprising. But the Utes were ready for them, ambushing them twenty miles from the White River agency. The battle raged for six days and by the time it was over the CO, Major T.T. Thornburgh and nine soldiers were dead, with forty-six wounded.

Two Fogs and his men had ridden to join in the attack so when Sheriff Greaves and his posse rode out of Dutch John the next day they met no opposition.

By high noon they had reached Bald Mountain and, as Greaves spotted the cliff overhang beneath a striped red mesa, where Mississippi Fred had said the two Easterners would be found, he raised his black-gloved hand and, with a downward motion of his fingers, indicated to the posse to stay quiet and hold back.

'C'mon, Shotgun,' he hissed, sliding from the saddle of his black bronc, 'Let's take a look. You others wait here. We don't want nobody else gittin' hurt.'

What he really wanted to do was see what these two were up to. If they had found a secret seam of gold, as he suspected, he didn't plan on sharing it with all and sundry. On foot, in his shiny boots, frock coat and black Stetson, he led the way, climbing up through the scree until he could peer down into the long cave. Completely unaware of their presence, Lucy Luffy was down on her knees scraping at something, while the professor was jotting down details in a book.

'All right, there,' Greaves barked out, his Smith & Wesson in his hand, 'hold it, you polecats. Don't make a move.'

'What on earth?' Lucy looked up. 'You nearly made me jump out of my skin!'

'Keep 'em covered, Shotgun.' Greaves stepped down to them, kicking curiously at one of several piles of what appeared to be bones. 'Shoot 'em down if they try anythang,' he drawled.

'Careful what you're doing, man,' Strangeways protested. 'Those piles are all carefully arranged and numbered.'

'Shut up. You're under arrest for the murder of George Larsen. Stick out your wrists. Come down here and cuff him, Gilligan.'

'Don't be ridiculous,' Strangeways said. 'Larsen and that other little runt, Fred, were about to rob and kill us both. It was self defence.'

'That's your story. I ain't so sure a jury'll see it your way. Come on, Shotgun, snap the irons on him.'

The burly Shotgun, in his dusty town suit, and derby hat, did so, frisking Strangeways and producing the 'storekeeper' from his pocket. 'There y'are, I told ya he was armed and dangerous. Is this the gun you used to kill Larsen?'

'It is, but — '

Shotgun cuffed him again, but this time with his fist, knocking the professor down on one knee.

'Leave him be, you fiends,' Lucy protested. 'He's speaking the truth.'

Sheriff Greaves gave his crooked grin as he regarded her. 'Like I say, that's for the jury to decide. Cuff her, too, Shotgun.'

'What? Leave me alone!' Lucy struggled as Shotgun grabbed hold of her, roughly, slapping her across the jaw, and locking the irons about her wrists. 'This is outrageous! You can't do this.'

'It's done. You're charged with treason. C'mon, we know all about you. You're one of them spies. The very least you're charged with, apart from accessory to homicide, is giving aid and comfort to rebel Indians. We got proof.'

'Don't be absurd. What proof?'

'Where's Dowson's musket?'

'I don't know. It went missing.'

'Yeah, into Two Fogs' arms. You been peddling weapons to the Utes, aincha, otherwise why did they let you live?'

'Two Fogs and I are old friends, but it is preposterous to say — '

'There y'a. Condemned outa her own mouth. So where's the gold?'

'What gold? We are merely digging up bones. Is that an offence? I might remind you we have the full backing of the Chicago Archaeological Museum and government approval. I'll have your badge for this, Sheriff.'

'Yeah, that's just a front. Go take a look, Shotgun.' He shoved Lucy back against the cliff wall. 'So who's the boss of this museum?'

'Professor Hyram Daniels. He is a man of immense stature in the East and a friend of the vice-president.'

'Yeah, tell that to the birds. This is the West, lady, and we do thangs different out here. Hey, what the hell's that?' He poked his boot at the huge skull half-dug from the soil. 'It's big, ain't it?'

'In plain English it's the skull of a dinosaur,' Lucy said, hotly. 'Now do you believe us? This is all we're interested in. So, why don't you two morons leave us alone to get on with our work.'

'Steady on, Lucy,' Matt muttered, 'that's no way to talk. Don't let's lose our tempers.'

'Oh, they make me sick,' she replied, as Shotgun Harry came trudging back along the wall of the cave.

'Cain't find no sign of a gold seam,' he called out. 'There's jest a load of funny-looking things stuck in the rock.'

'Don't touch them,' Lucy snapped. 'They are invaluable. Fossils, millions of years old.'

Greaves stroked his long, shaven jaw and frowned. 'What you mean, invaluable?'

'I mean they're priceless, a national treasure. You surely don't think we're excavating them for their monetary value, do you?'

'No? But, this stuff' — Greaves

indicated the finds — 'it must be worth somethang to somebody like, say, that Hyram Daniels?' He picked up the professor's fallen notebook and pencil. 'Just what is his address? I might need to get in touch with him, on your behalf, of course.'

When he had jotted the details down he took Shotgun to one side and spoke in a lowered voice. 'I figure we're on to somethang here. We could put the squeeze on this Hyram character. I reckon he wouldn't be averse to coughing up thousands in greenbacks for this li'l lot. We got to get rid of these two first, in a legal manner of course.' He grinned and drew his thumb across his throat. 'Let's git 'em back while the townsfolk are still braying for justice. We'll stir 'em up and let them do the dirty work.'

'This whole area ought to be put out-of-bounds to the general public,' the professor said, when they returned. 'We don't want people coming in here destroying valuable artefacts.'

'Thass OK,' Greaves said. 'I'll take care of that. Have you staked a claim on this cave yet?'

'No, of course not.'

'Well, I intend to, in my own name. That's the way we do it out here, Professor. I'll stake my claim at the claims office in Bonanza. All this will be legally mine to do with as I like.'

'Don't be so damned stupid,' Lucy snapped out.

Gilligan jabbed her with his shotgun. 'That's one thing the sheriff ain't, sister.' His ruddy face split into a broken-toothed grin. 'We got you two dingbats hogtied. You'll be headin' for the big goodbye. Then we'll be rich. Come on, move it, your ladyship.'

* * *

Dutch John was in an uproar. Settlers and their families had come in from their outlying farmsteads along the White and Green Rivers in fear of Ute vengeance. They packed the flour merchant's barn in which the trial was held. Greaves acted as presiding judge and chief prosecutor, sitting on a barrel in front of the crowd. He had paid out of his own pocket for several kegs of whiskey to be brought over from the saloon to be passed around and get the populace fired up.

'These two claim to be from some Chicago museum,' he drawled, lighting a cheroot, 'but in my opinion they're out to foment trouble among the tribes. Indirectly, they're responsible for the Meeker massacre.'

'He's mad. He's making this all up,' Lucy replied, hotly. 'If you people believe him you must be, too.'

She and the professor, in handcuffs, had been forced to stand before the crowd on a makeshift plank platform. 'It's quite simple to check our story,' Matt interjected. 'Just send a cable to the Chicago museum.'

'I am about to do that,' the sheriff replied, waving a form. 'Shotgun Harry, you take this, ride to Bonanza as fast as you can and cable this to Professor Daniels. We can't do fairer than that.'

'May I see that?' Lucy cried, but Shotgun had grabbed the form, and was striding out of the barn door and running for his horse. 'Oh, you fools, you don't believe him, do you? He's up to no good. In your parlance, your sheriff's as crooked as a wolf's leg.'

Matt winced, for Lucy's outspokenness was doing their case no good at all. The mood of the mob was getting uglier; they pressed forward, yelled insults.

'We ain't stupid out here,' a bearded man roared. 'Ain't it true you're a friend of Two Fogs? Just answer the question.'

'Well,' she faltered, 'yes, but — '

'She's been selling 'em guns,' the sheriff shouted, brandishing Dowson's Kentucky. 'Exhibit one.'

'Don't be — ' Lucy started, but was shouted down.

'When George Larsen and Mississippi Fred discovered what they were doing, under the pretext of scratching for bones, saw them trading with Two Fogs, when they rightly protested, that man Strangeways, shot Larsen in the back. And one of the Injins put an arrow in Mississippi. Ain't that so, Fred?'

'That's right.' The bandaged Mississippi had been carried in to sit beside the sheriff. He waved his crutch at the prisoners. 'Them two are equally guilty, in my book, of murdering poor George, God bless 'im.'

'He's a liar,' Lucy screamed, beginning to panic now. 'By the Lord's holy foreskin he's lying through his teeth. They both tried to murder me.'

'Listen to her blaspheme,' a woman settler shouted. 'She ain't wed to that man she's livin' with. How can we believe the words of a whore?'

'And a spy, too,' Greaves added, stirring them up. 'So, folks, who you gonna believe? Now's the time to cast your vote. Them who think these two ain't guilty of murder an' treason walk out the barn's back door. Them who believe she is go out the front door.'

'What sort of justice is this?' Lucy demanded. 'It's a travesty.'

'This is Western justice based on the old miners' law,' Greaves replied, taking a swig from the keg. 'Ain' no use you tryin' to confuse us with them long words. Us here are simple, honest folk.'

'Wait!' Panos Panayotis's wife arrived breathlessly, pushing through the throng. 'This lady is no murderer, nor is Professor Strangeways. They good people. I know. Believe me. You give them no chance to speak. It is Sheriff Greaves who is crook.'

Greaves growled at her, 'You be careful what you say.'

'If you are good people,' Mrs Panayotis cried, defiantly, 'you will follow me out of the back door.' In her black shawl and dress she appealed to them with her arms outstretched. 'Come. I go.' However, as she marched away out of the back, only one other woman followed her.

The sheriff gave a snigger and stroked his pencil moustache. 'You sensible folk know what the verdict should be. Those who say these two should suffer the lawful supreme punishment for murder, that is, hanging by the neck until they are dead, vote now.'

A gloomy silence came over the mob, but then, as one accord, they turned and began moving out of the wide front door. 'Let's string 'em up now,' a man shouted. 'This door beam's as good as any to hang 'em from.'

'Oh, God's toenails,' Lucy moaned. 'This is happening again.' It wasn't the first time she had faced a lynch mob. 'This is a nightmare.'

'Wait!' Sheriff Greaves stood up and fired his revolver into the roof, quieting the uproar. 'It's my duty to escort these two over to my jailhouse and hold 'em 'til I hear from Chicago.'

'No,' a woman screamed. 'Make 'em kick air now. Think of the Meekers!'

'Come on, you two,' the sheriff said,

turning his revolver on Lucy and Matt. 'Git movin'. It's for your own protection.'

Grim-faced, Lucy and Strangeways pushed their way through the crowd. They were jeered at and jostled, one woman spitting in Lucy's face. But Sheriff Greaves brandished his Smith & Wesson and got them through. 'Make way, folks,' he shouted. 'I got to do my lawful duty.'

Outside, however, he turned and said to one of the ringleaders of the mob, 'Of course, if you should come and take 'em yourselves while I'm over at the saloon having my supper, there ain't nuthin' I could do to stop you. I gen'rally leave the cell keys hanging on a hook just inside the office by my desk.'

He marched his prisoners away and slammed them into a cell, locking it. 'You can stay here while I go git you some eats,' he said, ignoring Lucy's pleas.

Outside, he looked across at the

crowd, still standing outside the barn, buzzing like a swarm of angry bees, as the big bearded man sent a rope snaking across the high beam above the open door, and turned to look across at the jailhouse, malevolently.

Greaves gave a thin-lipped smile and adjusted his Smith & Wesson beneath his frock coat. 'There ain't much you can do to stop a lynch mob once they got the bit between their teeth,' he drawled to nobody in particular, and strolled away along the street to the saloon.

8

The whiskey-bloated Jesse Greer, his bloody-bandaged foot hanging loose from the stirrup, had back-tracked his gang from Bonanza to try to fox the bounty hunters. The gang had heard some shooting in the hills the day before and had decided to ride into Dutch John to investigate. Jesse's foot was giving him grief and he was beginning to feel sweaty hot and feverish, so he planned to get the town doc to give it a look.

'We ain't got nuthin' to fear from the sheriff there, boys,' he said. 'He's as phoney as a three-dollar bill.'

They heard another shot echoing through the hills from Dutch John as they approached the town along the river-bank. 'Hang on, fellas, there's a rider comin' at the gallop. Scud and Wilk, git behind the rocks and keep him covered in case he gives us any lip.'

Shotgun Harry came belting along the trail in a cloud of dust, but hauled in when Jesse, Fee and Red pulled their horses across to block his path.

'Hold on, friend,' Jesse shouted. 'What's your hurry?'

'I gotta ride for Bonanza,' Shotgun shouted with self-importance. 'I'm the sheriff's deputy. I got a message to send. Out of my way.'

'Not so fast,' Red growled. 'What kind of message would that be?'

'I gotta send this cable to Chicago.' Shotgun patted his shirt pocket. 'We got a coupla dudes under sentence of death back in town and we need to know a few thangs.'

'Like what?' Red demanded.

'What business of that is yourn? Jest git out my way.'

'Hold on, friend,' Jesse put in, wiping a drip from his rosy nose and grinning at him. 'Would these two dudes be that young woman and a fella in spectacles? They reckoned they'd lost their cash and were out looking for bones?'

'That's them. But they murdered Big George and I figure the lynch mob will have them kickin' air before I git back.'

'Nuthin' like a good hangin'.' Jesse gave a roar of laughter. 'Maybe one day I'll be at my own.'

'You said it,' Red grinned. 'Mind if we take a look at that cable, mister?'

'It's private, between the sheriff and Chicago. Come on, I ain't got time to talk to you.' Shotgun Harry whupped his mustang across its neck with his reins and viciously spurred it to go, pushing through and racing on along the track.

Wilk Price took his time adjusting his sights, then took pressure on the Sharps' trigger. The shot cracked out. Shotgun threw up his arms as he was hit in the back and toppled from his horse into the dust.

'Good shootin', Wilk,' Jesse called. 'Must be all of a hundred yards. Thought you were leavin' it a bit late. Red, go git that cable and anything else of value he might have.'

When Red returned with the form, and tucking Shotgun's cash into his own pocket, Jesse took it from him and called out, 'Hey, Wilk, you can figure out words, caincha? Come here and read this.'

Wilk studied it. It was addressed to some professor at the Chicago museum.

HAVE LADE CLAIM TO DYNERSAW'S HEAD AND OTHER BONES STOP IF YOU WANT THEM SEND BANKER'S DRAFT TO ME FUR TWENTY THOUSAND DOLLARS KASHABLE AT GRAND JUNKSHUN BANK STOP ACT PRONTO OR FINDS WILL BE DESTROID STOP PEE ESS LUFFY AND STRANGEWAYS SENTENCED TO DEATH FOR HOMICIDE STOP I AM HOLDING THEM IN JAIL PENDING YOUR REPLY STOP YOURS TRULY STOP SHERIFF LUKE GREAVES STOP DUTCH JOHN STOP COLORADO STOP OR WE MIGHT BE IN UTAH STOP I AIN'T SURE.

'What in tarnation's he talking about, dinosaur's heads and bones?' Jesse asked, with a smirk. 'Strikes me the sheriff's been imbibing too much whiskey. How can a few bones be worth twenty thousand dollars? He's gawn plumb crazy.'

He was about to crumple the cablegram and toss it away when Wilk said, 'Hold on, Jess. I agree a heap of bones cain't be worth much, but them two scientists? Wouldn't their lives be worth something to this guy at the Chicago museum?'

'Duh, Pa,' Scud giggled. 'What's he talkin' bout?'

'You listen to Wilk, boy, and you might learn somethang. He's the only one of you lot with a brain in his box. Wilk's got a point. What he means is, we kidnap these two birds and hold 'em to ransom. Ain't that so, Wilk?'

'That's right. A ransom of, say, twenty thousand dollars. OK?'

'Yee-ho!' Red slapped his hat across

Scud's head. 'Boys, you hear that, we gonna git rich.'

'First we got to reword this cable,' Wilk said, fishing a pencil stub out of his shirt pocket. 'What shall I say? To the same bozo in Chicago, etcetera. We have Luffy and Strangeways safe. Stop. Send 20,000 dollars to Green River town bank, Utah, payable to — let me see — J. Greer, and they will be returned alive. Stop. Otherwise they git shot.' He was using Red's back to write on, and now presented it to him with a flourish. 'Ride to Bonanza post haste and send this. We'll wait for you with the captives at the old cabin in Crazy Woman Creek.'

'Yeah.' Red snatched the cable eagerly, but had second thoughts. 'Hey, what if I bump into those bounty hunters?'

'Aw, they'll be miles away by now,' Jesse beamed. 'We gonna need all four of us to rescue them two dudes 'fore they git hanged. And my guess is we better act fast. Go on, Red, ride hard.

This beats robbin' banks. There'll be fair shares for all, boys, when the twenty thou' comes through.'

As Red charged away, the others turned their mounts and, leaving Shotgun Harry's body by the trail, headed like a pack of hungry wolves towards Dutch John.

'Remember, boys,' Jesse growled, 'we git any trouble, shoot first and ask questions after.'

* * *

'I'm sorry to have got you into this, Matt.' Lucy Luffy spoke in a strangulated voice as the hempen necktie was given a jerk and tightened alarmingly. 'I think I should have taken your advice and gone home.'

'Now she tells me,' Strangeways muttered, as, still hand-cuffed, he was forced to mount a plank balanced on two barrels and stand beside her as a noose was slipped over his own head. 'It looks like we'll soon find out the big secret, whether there's life on t'other side or not. In a way, I'm glad to be going with you, Lucy. You see, I love you.'

'Now he tells me,' she replied.

The big, bearded ringleader of the mob pulled both ropes, snaked over the oakbeam entrance to the barn, tight so that both prisoners had to stand teetering on tiptoes. The crowd of settlers had fallen quiet now their time was due and the big man called, 'You got any last words you want to say?'

'Yes, go book yourself in an asylum, you lunatic. You're all completely mad.'

'She's right. This is nothing to do with her,' Matt pleaded. 'Hang me, but you will be committing cold-blooded murder if you — '

'That's enough.' The big man went to kick the plank away. Wilk Price sat his horse fifty yards away and took aim. The Sharps buffalo gun belched flame and the rope above Lucy's head was cut in twain.

'Good Lord,' she said, feeling the

loose rope drop onto her shoulders. 'Hold on, Matt. Maybe He does exist.'

However, Strangeways was not so lucky. Wilk calmly reloaded the Sharps and took aim again, as the lynch mob shouted and women screamed and scattered in alarm. Wilk took second pressure on the trigger but at that moment his horse shied and instead of cutting Matt's rope, the bullet ploughed into the belly of the big man.

The bearded settler toppled forward and knocked over the plank and barrels before he slowly expired, flapping like a landed fish in the dust. Lucy tumbled on top of him with a squawk of alarm. The rope twanged tightly around Strangeways throat and he was kicking his last.

Lucy scrambled to her feet, cupping her hand-cuffed arms under her friend's shoes, trying to take the pressure and hold him aloft, but his eyes were bulging and his tongue was protruding from his throat.

Scud Greer charged his bronc in and

slashed the rope with his knife, swirling the mustang around, knocking people over like ninepins, and looking down at the fallen man. 'Aw, too bad, Pa, he's gawn,' he shouted.

'Never mind, boy.' Jesse ambled his horse up towards the mob, his long-barrelled Buntline Special pointing skywards. 'Grab hold of the gal. She'll have to suffice.'

Lucy was down on her knees, slapping at Matt's face, trying to bring him round, but it looked as if he'd gone. And then she felt another lariat noose drop over her shoulders, and tighten, and she was jerked off her feet, dragged along the street. 'What are you doing?' she screamed

Jesse Greer adjusted his Lincoln hat with his left hand and grinned down at her. 'You'll soon find out, sister.'

Luke Greaves had been watching the hangings from across the way, standing on the sidewalk outside the Longhorn saloon, pretending they were nothing to do with him. 'What 'n hell's goin' on?'

he whispered, licking at his lips.

'It's the Greers,' a settler shouted, as the bearded, scrawny Fee, in his floppy hat and caped coat, rode his mustang into them, yelling and whooping, making them back away into the barn. Scud giggled and joined him in the fun, crashing off his revolver, sending bullets whistling over the mob's head.

Jesse gave the rope around Lucy a jerk and pulled her onto her feet, making her run along behind him as he jogged on his horse towards the crowd. 'Yes, it's us,' he snarled, sourly, his foot aching so much he felt as angry as a grizzly with a sore head. 'I guess us Greers is makin' quite a name for ourselves. No use sayin' we ain't. Right, you miserable bastards. I bet you don't feel so brave now. Fancy trying to hang this poor innocent girl. We've saved her life and we're taking her with us so you cain't do her no more harm. You better git back to your farmsteads. Anybody comes after us it will be the worse for them.'

Sheriff Greaves's mouth had gone dry and he felt a sudden emptiness inside. He was not a man who liked to fight against the odds, preferring to shoot a fellow in the back if he could. And now he was left without Shotgun Harry to side him things did not look good. To see Greer's gunmen taking over the town made his legs weak and sent a shiver up his spine. He was in half a mind to turn tail, make a run for his horse, but it was too late. Jesse Greer had spotted him.

'Well, by Jehosophat,' he jeered, 'ain't that your noble sheriff?'

'Yeah, Greaves,' one of the onlookers called, 'what you going to do about this? Why don't you arrest these gunmen? We'll have ourselves a proper hanging.'

Greaves swallowed his fear. 'You must be joking,' he muttered.

'Come here, Greavsey.' Jesse grinned, evilly, and beckoned him with the Buntline. 'Don't be shy.'

For moments the sheriff froze, but

with the whole town populace staring at him expectantly, it seemed there was nothing left to do but step slowly down from the saloon and walk across the dusty street towards Greer and the other rampaging outlaws.

'Hiya, Mr Greer,' he said, pausing ten feet away from the patriarch and giving an oily smile. 'Nice to see you. Welcome to our town.'

'Welcome, huh! If I turned my back you'd waste no time about shooting me down. I heard about you, Luke Greaves. Nuthin' but a murdering, cheating swine. You oughta be ashamed to wear that badge.'

'Don't be like that, Jesse,' Luke wheedled. 'You know, maybe I'm all washed up here. Maybe I could join you boys. I'm pretty fast with a gun.'

'You are, are you? Well, I ain't sure I want a rattlesnake like you ridin' along with us. We're God-fearin' Missouri boys. What I want to know is, you got a sawbones in Dutch John?'

'Sure, Jesse. Doc Flanders. Got a

cabin on the edge of town. Why, you in trouble?'

'Ain't none of your business.'

'What you gonna do with the gal, Jesse? Mebbe, if I came along I could help you with her.'

'My interest in the young lady is purely a humanitarian one,' Jesse replied, in the highflown manner he affected at times. 'To save her from you scum.'

Unbeknown to him, one of the settlers had edged away from the crowd behind his wagon and was reaching for his carbine hidden beneath some sacking. He levered it and cracked out a shot at Greer. The bullet sent his top hat flying. Jesse whirled his big horse, extended his arm full-length with the Buntline and crashed out a shot that catapulted the settler back into a horse trough.

'Thass right, have a good drink,' Jesse laughed, putting another slug in his back for good measure. 'It's the last you'll have.'

'Watch out, Pa!' Scud yelled a warning.

Luke Greaves had panicked, deciding that his chances were minimal unless he acted fast. His gloved right hand had snaked over beneath his frock coat to the holstered Smith & Wesson on his right thigh and whipped it out. But, in his panic, he fired too fast, and, as the self-cocker expelled its lead, missed Jesse by inches.

The sheriff went for a second shot but the revolver was smashed from his palm and he screamed as blood spurted from a hole through his hand. Wilk Price had had him in his rifle's sights and this time had not missed.

Jesse Greer grinned as he turned to peer at the sheriff, who was hanging on to his wounded hand in obvious agony. 'Nice try, Greavsey,' he said, and his Buntline blasted the gambler into extinction. 'You got a poor hand.' His pun greatly amused him and he appealed to the crowd: 'Geddit?'

No, they apparently did not, staring

at him in silent bemusement as the acrid black powder smoke rolled, wondering who was to be next victim.

'Look at this lot,' Scud giggled. 'Like a lot of forlorn chickens on a wet day. Shall we kill 'em?'

'No, two's enough. I got me a terrible headache. All this noise. Let's go find that quack.' Jesse glanced at the prone Strangeways. 'He ain't no use to nobody. We'll just take the girl.'

He turned his horse and sauntered it away, jerking the lariat so Lucy had no option but to follow him.

'Oh, God's teeth,' she sobbed, 'what is he planning to do to me?' It was like the old saying, out of the frying pan into the fire.

'You boys,' Jesse yelled back. 'Pick up some supplies and some whiskey. Join me at the cabin. Make sure you got plenty of stuff. We're headed on a long journey.'

9

Red Griffin strolled out of the telegraph office in Bonanza feeling pleased with himself. The old guy in his green eyeshade had tapped out the cable to Chicago. He looked somewhat quizzical but asked no questions. Twenty thousand smackeroos! Good old Wilk. Trust him to come up with an idea like that. Red was excited at the prospect of getting rich quick. Now to get back to the cabin in Crazy Woman Creek.

But Red had a thirst. He glanced, narrow-eyed, along the street of dilapidated false fronts. It was all quiet in the afternoon heat. Not much going on in the stores. An old-timer whittling in the shade of the sidewalk. Was it likely anybody would recognize Red? What did it matter? The sheriff was defunct. Even if they did spot him he could handle these panhandling deadbeats.

Red jerked his hat down to cover his rusty hair, and flexed the powerful muscles beneath his plaid shirt. He loosened the Colt Navy .36 in the holster, and led his horse along the dusty street. It looked more like a ghost town than ever now. He hitched it outside the Palace of Varieties, and jumped on to the raised sidewalk, stomping in his heavy boots through the batwing doors. He stood, his eyes becoming accustomed to the gloom, assessing the occupants. There were a couple of desultory card games in progress, a few farmers who glanced up and went back to their game. The three whores were sprawled on the horsehair sofa fanning themselves. Why worry about them?

There was no one at the bar to serve him. 'What do I do?' he shouted. 'Help myself?'

Wandering Hands Wanda detached herself from her colleagues and ambled across in her sweat-sticky eelskin dress. 'Don't I know you?' she squawked.

'Maybe you do, maybe you don't, pigface. Maybe it would be advisable to have a short memory. Just gimme a beer an' you won't git no trouble.'

Wanda shrugged, listlessly. ''Pigface? Huh! You wanna look in a mirror sometime.' She filled a tankard with beer and sent it sliding along the mahogany top to his outstretched hand. She leaned on the bar and watched Red sink it in one. 'That's fifty cents.'

'Gimme another.' He sent the glass sliding back and she filled it again and repeated the process. 'Thanks.' He flicked her a cartwheel dollar.

Wanda caught it and tested it in her teeth. 'So, what brings you back to town? The bank's closed down. You looking for some action of a more intimate kind? Only this time you gotta behave yourself.'

Red supped the second beer more slowly, and grinned at her. 'Maybe I could. I got ten minutes to spare.'

'Come on then, darlin'.' Wanda waddled away and climbed the stairs.

On the balcony she turned and called, 'I'm waitin' for ya.'

Red pushed his glass aside and took the stairs two at a time, following Wanda into a bedroom and slamming the door. A few minutes later Jim Roland, followed by Hank and Chris, pushed through the swing doors and, spurs jingling, approached the bar.

'My, oh my,' the skinny Swede, Helga, sang out and sprang to her feet. 'How can I help you gentlemen? You looking for liquor or a good time? You better answer quick 'cause us girls are gettin' rushed off our feet.'

Jim Roland laid his hat Aside and ran fingers through his thick mop of blond hair. He imagined she was being sarcastic because there didn't appear to be much happening at all in Bonanza. 'You got any bourbon left?'

'For you, handsome, anything.' Helga smiled, and pulled a bottle out from under the counter. 'Shall I put it on the bill? Maybe you'd like to split it with me upstairs?'

'Not today, Josephine.' Roland raised an eyebrow at Hank and Chris and poured three slugs. 'We're still on the trail of those bank robbers, the Greers, but we ain't had much luck. You seen any sign of them?'

Helga smiled again, mischievously, and rubbed her thumb and forefinger. 'That would be telling, wouldn't it?'

'Don't beat about the bush,' Hank growled. 'Have you or haven't you?'

'We're always ready to pay for information,' Roland said, studying the bourbon, and taking a bite of it. He pulled his fringed buckskin jacket aside and took a bank wad from his shirt pocket, peeling off a note. 'How about a five spot?'

'How about ten and I'll toss myself in for good measure.'

'You and your info would have to be pretty good for that much. Five is all. How about it?'

Suddenly Helga saw Red come out on to the balcony, jerking his gunbelt tight. She quickly reached out and snatched up the five, whispering, 'He's all yours, honey. Look behind you.'

Roland followed the direction of her eyes, his hand sliding to the hickory grip of his Lightning on his right hip as he spun around. But Red had seen him and his Navy .36 was out already spitting lead. 'Aagh!' Chris cried, as he caught the bullet between the eyes and crumpled to the floorboards. Hank dived for cover as Jim stood his ground and, stretched out his arm with care to send three slugs smashing into the woodwork of the bedroom walls. Red was moving away along the balcony, his .36 coughing flame and lead. Suddenly he pirouetted, clutching his chest as Jim caught him with a heart shot. His eyes bulged as he staggered forward and pitched over the banister. His corpse crashed on to the table of the card players below, demolishing it.

'Any *more* of them?' Roland yelled at Helga who had dived for cover behind the bar.

'No,' she screamed. 'He's the only

one. At least the only one who's come in here.'

'There was only one hoss hitched,' Hank remarked, picking himself up from behind the roulette table. 'Good shootin', Jim.'

'Chris is dead.' Roland shook his head as he glanced at his blood-oozing colleague. 'He didn't have a chance.'

'He knew the odds,' Hank muttered, his gun in hand, turning it from one to the other present. 'That's how it goes in this game.'

'He was a good man.' Roland, too, was alert, his gun poised, ready for any more trouble, the adrenalin pumping through his body. 'We were careless there.'

'Still, at least and at last,' Hank said, as he went and poked at Red's body with his boot, 'we got one of the varmints. That means the others can't be far away. There's a five hundred dollars reward on this one.'

'Yep.' Jim Roland holstered his Lightning and took another slug of the bourbon. 'It's a start.'

People had come running to see what the commotion was about, including the ancient telegraph operator. 'Jeez,' he cried, staring down at Red. 'I just sent a cable off for that feller to Chicago. He wanted twenty thousand sent to the bank at Green River to be paid to somebody called Wilk Price, or else they git it.'

'Who gets it?' Roland asked.

The old man stroked his chin, 'Let's see, what was their names?'

'Come on, grandad,' Jim snapped out. 'Would it have been Miss Luffy and Professor Strangeways?'

'Luffy and Strangeways, that's them.'

'Have a drink, old-timer,' Jim Roland said, pushing the bottle across. 'Come on, Hank. Go give the undertaker five dollars to bury Chris. We gotta be moving out.'

'He'll be needing another five dollars,' Helga called out from the veranda. She had gone up to take a look at Wanda. 'She's dead. The bullets went right through the bedroom wall.'

'Aw, shee-it.' Jim placed another five note on the bar. 'Come on, Hank, let's go.'

* * *

The packrats had taken over the cabin in Crazy Woman Creek. It was reputed to be haunted so folks gave it a wide berth. That was to the liking of the Greer gang. But the rats didn't like being ousted and kept climbing back in the open windows to see what they could find. For the moment the outlaws had their minds on other matters for Jesse's shrieks were fit to wake the dead.

'Sit on his head, Scud,' Wilk shouted, as he and Fee tried to hang on to Jesse's desperately kicking legs. They had poured whiskey into the fat old Missouri raider, but it only made him kick the more, like he was dangling on the end of a rope.

'Hold him still,' Doc Flanders cried,

as he tried to extract what remained of Jesse's big toenail with a pair of pincers, and trimmed the raw flesh of the stub with scissors. 'How can I get at him?'

The diminutive doctor had a bad case of the shakes, his hand trembling as he wiped sweat from his eyes and took a break. 'Pass me that whiskey, for God's sake.'

The handcuffed Lucy, her dress torn and dust-grimed, squatted in a corner of the cabin and watched. The medic appeared to be in the throes of delirium tremens, or perhaps he was terrified of being shot if anything went wrong. Some desperate glugs at the bottle calmed him and he went back to work. 'Hang on, boys, I got to try to stitch the bits of skin together if I can. It's a wonder this ain't gone gangrenous by now.'

A packrat was hopping along the side of the wall towards the girl, its beady eyes gleaming. But he was after Wilk's watch, the chain of which was hanging out of the outlaw's back pocket. The rats were fascinated by shiny objects and great hoarders. He jerked the chain in his teeth and, as the watch tumbled out, scampered away and out of the doorway.

'Make sure that bit of wood's still 'tween his teeth, Scud,' Fee shouted. 'Or he'll bite his tongue off.'

'Aw,' Scud giggled, 'who cares? It'd make a change if Pa didn't have nuthin' to say.'

Jesse had lapsed into silence, screwing up his eyes to try to stop unmanly tears flowing as the quack stitched with a needle and gut at his toe. But when Flanders dosed it with iodine he hollered like a banshee. 'Woe-uh is me,' he groaned.

'That's all I can do.' The doc reached for the bottle again. 'Except bandage it up. He oughta rest. If he rides his hoss the jolting is just goin' to aggravate the wound.'

'Let him up,' Wilk growled, when the bandaging was done. He began to pull on his tattered topcoat and felt in his back pocket. 'Hey, who's stolen my watch?'

'A rat took it,' Lucy informed him. 'Poetic justice, really. No doubt you stole it yourself, so it's gone from one thieving rat to another.'

'You shut your mouth, sister.' Wilk glowered at her. 'Or I'll be shutting it for you.'

'Yeah,' Fee turned to stare at her. 'I bet she's one of them smartasses who don't believe in God, claims we're all descended from baboons.'

'No, I think in your case more probably rats.'

'Duh? She's real askin' for it.' Scud leered at her with his deformed mouth. 'When we goin' to give it her, boys?'

'We ain't got time for that. We got to get outa here fast,' Wilk snapped. 'But I can assure you, honey, you're gonna git a good stiff talkin' to from me just as soon as we've put space 'tween us and them who might be on our tail. C'mon, boys, let's ride.'

'What about Pa?' Scud howled. 'He

cain't ride in his state. He's just had a serious operation. And he's still pig drunk.'

'Boys.' Doc Flanders was twitching at Wilk's sleeve. 'There's the matter of my fee. I've done a good job.'

'Aw, git lost, you li'l squirt. Think yourself lucky we don't shoot you. If you can catch that rat you can keep my watch.' Wilk turned to look at the perspiring Jesse Greer. 'If he cain't ride that's too bad. We'll have to leave him.'

'No.' Scud picked up Jesse's Buntline and waggled it at Wilk. 'No way am I leavin' my pa.'

'Why not make a raft?' Fee suggested. 'The way that current races we'll git down to Green River faster than goin' by horseback. We can buy new broncs with all that dough that's comin' to us at Green River bank.'

'Thass a good idea, Fee,' Scud said, grinning foolishly. 'C'mon, let's go make a start. Fancy him wantin' to leave Pa after all he's done for us.'

'OK, seems I'm out-voted.' Wilk

pointed at Jesse. 'But as soon as we git to Green River you're on your own. I ain't carryin' no invalids.'

'Aw, Wilk, don' be like that,' Jesse slurred, looking dazed but cheerful that the worst of the pain was gone. 'I'll be all right in a coupla days.'

Wilk went over to Lucy, unlocked one of her wrists with the dead sheriff's keys, dragged her over to Jesse and locked the spare handcuff to his wrist. 'There, now you got company, Jesse. She tries to go anywhere she's gonna have to drag you along, too. Keep an eye on her. Make sure she don't get up to no monkey tricks.' He took the Buntline from Scud and stuffed it in his belt. 'I'll take this so she don't git her paws on it if Jesse passes out.'

'He thinks of everything, doesn't he?' Lucy smiled sweetly at Jesse when Wilk was gone. 'Aren't you supposed to be the leader of this gang? You're surely aware he's planning to get the money for himself and ditch you?'

Jesse stared at her angrily and

snorted. 'Don't try stirring me up, missy. It won't work. We're brothers-in-arms. The same clan. All for one and one for all.'

'You hope,' she said. 'If I were you, Jesse, I'd get rid of that Wilk. He's dangerous.'

A couple of hours later, the boys returned to hoist Jesse up on their backs, dragging Lucy along down to the river. They had, she saw, made a solid enough raft of timbers and rope. 'Come on,' Wilk said. 'Load up the saddles and bridles and leave the broncs. Lay Jesse down there. You beside him, bitch.'

They poled away into deep water and on round the first of many bends in the river on its journey south. When dusk fell they just kept going guided by the moonlit gleam of the river. There was little sound but for the splash and gurgle of the water, the occasional shrill cry of a waterfowl. Lucy lay and watched the somewhat ghostly scene, the hunched shapes of the men bearing her away, the silhouettes of trees on the banks as they passed and, suddenly, a ranch house fire, flames licking into the night sky. The Utes were out and busy bringing terror. Since the lynching of poor Matt and in spite of the wonderful finds they had half-unearthed, a deep sense of dread had begun to gnaw at Lucy, a regret that she set out on this unfortunate expedition. How, she wondered, could she possibly escape from these ignorant psychopaths. There was little chance, she knew, whether a ransom was paid or not, that she would get out of this alive.

10

'It looks like the birds have flown the coop.' James Roland pointed to the deep tracks in the sand of the river-bank where a raft had been hauled into the water. 'See those smaller bootprints? They've got the girl with them, that's for sure.'

'That's gonna be a problem, ain't it?' Hank replied. 'We won't just be able to go hog-wild with the lead when we catch up with 'em. Shall we go into Dutch John and see what's been going on?'

'No, we haven't got time for that.' Roland swung up onto Rajah. 'We need to get to Green River before them. Every second counts.'

But, even in two days of hard riding, going at a hard lope across rocky terrain and keeping as close to the river as they could, they had still not seen a glimpse of the raft. They were lucky to cover fifty miles a day for it was tough going and they needed to feed and rest their horses at night.

'This don't look good,' Hank said, as they trailed into the Cameron ranch. The settler in question was hanging by his bootheels from a cottonwood branch over the smouldering ruins of his ranch house. Nearby, were the corpses of his wife and young daughter, their bodies bristling with arrows like human pincushions. 'At least they ain't been scalped or tortured. They died quick.'

'Cut him down, Hank.' Roland jogged his horse away around the stark and grisly scene, its eeriness added to by the sunset's afterglow. A Ute warrior was sprawled dead. They were a tribe not believed to be as cruel as the Apache or Comanche, but all men could be vengeful in war. They had not had it all their own way. Cameron had died fighting. The raiding party had run off what horses and cattle they could find. The pigs were still in their sty. Most Indians regarded them as reincarnated devils and would not eat them. Roland opened their gate and let them out. Better they run wild than die of starvation. Chickens, too, were clucking around, running in and out of the still burning barn. The bounty hunter picked up an incinerated one, all her feathers burned off. He took it back and tossed it down. 'Ready cooked supper,' he said.

When they had buried the Camerons and fixed wood and string crosses on the graves, they gutted the chicken and ate her flesh which was a tad burnt, but tasty, and settled down to rest against their saddles. It was unlikely the Utes would return. Jim had found a tin of lard in an unburned part of the kitchen and used it to grease his copper-jacketed bullets, and the cylinders of his revolver and carbine. A touch in his gunbelt holster might save his life, too.

'It's a macabre scene,' he muttered, looking at the charred skeleton of the ranch house, which still flickered flames amid its black and red ash. 'But the fire sure takes away the night chill. I wonder how she's coping.'

'She's a tough cookie, it struck me,' Hank replied, as he rolled a cigarette. 'The kinda gal would suit you, Jim, you once being an officer and gentleman.'

'That seems a long time ago now. No, you couldn't expect a woman like that to hitch up with a hired killer, as she called me. But I must admit I was smitten by Miss Lucy Luffy.'

'It must have been hard in military prison, weren't it, Jim? You being a former captain.'

'Yeah, all t'others were enlisted men, so I did get singled out for special treatment by some of the tougher types with a chip on their shoulders. However, I survived. But, I tell you something, Hank, I came out a different man than I went in after two years breaking rocks.'

'Waal, you need to be hard and emotionless in our occupation. It ain't wise to make a buddy of your partner. If he gits the chop like Chris it hits you hard. He was a quiet spoken feller. I could never fathom him out, either. Something had gone wrong in his life. Me, I just enjoy the job and the cash that comes along.'

'We ain't made much so far,' Roland sighed. 'This has been a real ornery assignment. Now they've got the girl it complicates it more.'

'Never mind, Jim,' Hank cackled. 'I've noticed you never spend your cash on the doxies in the saloons. But I believe you need a woman to relax with. A man cain't be tensed like a spring all the time. Maybe this'll be your lucky case. The way she was hanging on to you when you two were dancing I figure she was smitten by you, too. Once we get her back she's gonna be mighty grateful to you, boy.'

'Let's face the facts, Hank. It's unlikely the Greers will let her live once they've had their filthy hands on her.

And, anyway, what decent woman wants to get mixed up with an ex-con? No, a bounty hunter's no right even to dream of a wife and children. So, let's get a coupla hours' shut-eye, shall we, 'fore we head on.'

*   *   *

Although it was difficult to hazard a guess, Lucy Luffy figured that they must have covered a hundred miles along the sharply meandering river. The small settlement of Green River, before the Green River itself wound onwards towards the canyon of the Colorado, couldn't be far now.

'Aagh!' Jesse cried, as the raft hit a submerged rock and spun around. He jerked her wrist, hand-cuffed to his. 'My foot! Come on, boys, pole us ashore. Let's take a rest.'

'You been resting on your back two days next to that dame, Pa,' Scud yelled. 'What you moaning about? I figure it's my turn.'

'Oh, God,' Lucy prayed. 'Keep him away from me.'

But, at least it was good to stretch her arms and legs, as Wilk unlocked their wrists, and to scramble ashore. 'Can I have a little privacy?' she asked. 'I have to go into the bushes.'

'Dur!' Scud slavered. 'I better keep a watch on you.'

'Leave her, boy,' Jesse ordered. 'A lady like her don't want you sniffing around her when she's doin' her ablutions. Come here, help me hop across to sit against that rock. What would your dear departed mother think of you, the Lord bless her soul. You need to show a li'l respect for womanhood.'

'What a load of sentimental bull, Jesse,' Wilk snapped. 'You know you strangled that wife of yourn.'

'I wasn't aware of what I was doing,' the grey-bearded Jesse wailed, making the sign of the cross. 'The devil's brew was in me. She shoulda known better'n to nag me. Got me het up. But Satan guided my hands that day. I spent the rest of my life regrettin' it. Such a dear, sweet woman, she was.'

'Come off it, Jesse,' Fee sneered. 'She weren't nothing but a miserable old termagant. What a mouth she had on her. Never stopped. You did the world a favour, mister.'

During this to-and-fro, as they automatically set about making camp in the sandy cove, Scud had disappeared. Meanwhile, Lucy had done what was necessary and was knelt further up the river splashing at her hands and face, trying to tidy herself. Suddenly, she gave a scream as Scud landed on top of her. His weight was impossible to escape from although she kicked and struggled as his dirt-engrained hands tore at her dress and groped at her. He was giggling, maniacally, slobbering over her face, trying to kiss her. 'I'm gonna have you, bitch,' Scud panted, as he forced himself between her thighs. 'I'm gonna give you somethang to remember me by.'

Lucy panicked, trapped by his bulk and strength, unable to escape. Her hands touched the back of his obese waist; his leather belt; his knife in its scabbard! She gripped its haft in her right hand, took a deep breath, slipped it out, raised it as high as she could reach and, with all her strength, brought the razor-sharp steel down to stab into his back. 'Get off me, you fiend!' she screamed, and twisted the knife, pulled it out, and sliced it into the half-wit's flesh again.

Scud groaned and flailed his arms, trying to grab at her throat. Lucy stabbed him repeatedly until he ceased, then rolled his carcass away with a sob of disgust. 'It serves you right,' she said, as she saw his fleshy, pimply face taughten in a rictus of pain and sudden death.

'What in hell's going on?' Fee was first on the scene and stared at her as if he could hardly believe his eyes. 'Jesse, she's killed him! She's killed Scud!'

'What?' Jesse roared, and came

hobbling along on a makeshift crutch. He, too, stood for moments as if struck down. Then he howled to the heavens. 'The bitch has kilt him! She's kilt my dear boy who never harmed anyone in this world!'

Her arm and dress soaked with blood, Lucy Luffy lay beside Scud's corpse, almost as shocked as they were, staring up at the three kin. They had cold anger burning in their eyes and Jesse was pulling out his Buntline and thumbing the hammer, it's deathly hole pointed at her forehead. There was nothing she could do. This, she knew, was it. The only thought that passed through her head was, What a waste of time it has all been. I had so much work to do . . .

'The Lord will take vengeance for this,' Jesse was ranting, 'an eye for an eye . . .'

Suddenly, from the crag above them came the crack of a carbine shot and, at the same instant, a bullet ploughed into Jesse's chest, bowling him over. He lay on his back in the rocks and water, staring at them, vainly pleading, 'Help me, boys. Help me up.'

But Wilk and Fee were too busy dodging for cover to bother with the old man as a fusillade of lead whistled and whined about their heads from above.

The cliff was too steep-sided to climb up or down, and from his position at the top Jim Roland fed more bullets into the magazine of his Winchester and peered down. 'I got that fat barrel of lard, Greer,' he gritted out. 'Looks like he's finished. For Christ's sake get out of the way, run for it, girl.'

But 250 feet down below Lucy was still too shocked and stunned to know what to do, except try to crawl forward and extricate Jesse Greer's big Buntline from his hands.

'Where are them other two var-mints?' Hank asked, leaving the cover of his rock up above to try to get a better view down below.

'Get back, Hank,' Roland hissed. 'Don't show yourself.'

'Where they got to?'

They were the last words he spoke. Wilk Price had him in the sights of his long-barrelled buffalo gun. The Sharps barked flame and Hank suddenly spun in his tracks as the big bullet hit him. He teetered for seconds on the cliff edge then plunged down to smash on to the rocks and sprawl lifeless.

'Hot damn.' Jim Roland cursed, and furiously released a torrent of lead at the whereabouts of the two men below until his magazine was empty again and the carbine smoking in his hands. 'You durn fool, Hank.'

Lucy had just got the Buntline in her hands when Wilk Price dodged back under the cover of the rocks and hauled her to her feet by the scruff of her dress. He bludgeoned her forearm with the Sharps, knocking the Buntline into the river water.

'You're coming with us,' he snarled, as she cried out with pain, and he swung her body around to use as a shield. 'Get the raft back in the water,

Fee. Quick, while he's reloading. We're getting outa here.' He whispered in Lucy's ear as he backed away, dragging her with him, 'We ain't finished with you, darlin'. You're my passport outa here.'

By the time Fee had hauled the raft out into the current, Jim Roland had his Winchester ready to fire again. Wilk Price was standing on the prow of the log contraption, looking up at the cliff, but with Lucy held tight in front of him.

Fee was struggling in panic to jump aboard the rear of the raft as he set it moving again so Roland did the only thing he could, levering a slug into the breech and taking him out. Fee gasped and raised his arms as if in surrender as blood curdled out of his back and he slowly slid into the embrace of the river.

'Damn you.' The bounty hunter watched as the raft slowly drifted on its way. Just before rounding a bend and being lost to sight, Price in an ironic manner waved his long rifle at him.

Roland chewed on a slice of baccy he still had in his mouth and spat out the juice over the cliffside. 'What'll I do now?' he asked himself.

He climbed back up the cliff and made his way along to where they had hitched their horses. He jumped on to Rajah's back and carefully manoeuvred him along the treacherous cliffside, peering down at the winding river for any sign of the raft. 'Price needn't think I'm finished yet,' he muttered. 'I got Hank to avenge for a start.'

Fury against the gunman and tense worry about the girl was battling for possession. 'Careful,' he said, as the powerful horse slipped, but regained balance. 'We don't want to do nothing silly.'

There was a strange sound coming from beyond another bend in the river which, as he cantered Rajah along the clifftop, gradually intensified in volume. 'Hell's Kitchen,' he shouted, remembering the name of the rapids and falls that were looming up. The sheen and whorl of water was entering a narrow chasm of steep sided walls and consequently increasing the speed and power of its flow. Roland could see that a raft wouldn't have a chance if it went over. It, and whoever was on it, would be smashed to pieces on black, jagged rocks and whirlpools below.

He bit his lip with worry and indecision, then bent Rajah around and cantered back the way he had come until the raft came into view. It was beginning to go at a faster pace as Price poled it towards the narrow gorge. Soon it began tossing and spinning around. He could hear Lucy's scream as she hung on.

'Now,' he whispered, pulling the Winchester from the boot and hugging it into his shoulder as he sat Rajah. Now was his only chance. He squeezed out a bullet but it was a long shot for a carbine, only succeeding in making Price duck down and stare up to locate the shootist. He immediately grabbed the girl and dragged her body back to cover him.

'Hell,' Roland cursed again. 'I shoulda waited. The fool's gonna go over. He's gonna take her with him.'

For seconds he sat there, transfixed with horror. Then he thrust the Winchester back in the boot, and spurred Rajah racing back along the clifftop towards a dip where he would be only 100 feet above them. 'Hyah!' Jim yelled, choosing his take-off spot, whipping the horse around and forward and then leaped Rajah into space . . . and they were falling, air sucked from them, the wall of water coming up fast. It hit them with a massive jolt, and they were sinking and sinking, the bounty hunter keeping his feet caught in the bentwood stirrups, holding his breath as, in a kind of slow motion, the kicking horse, its mane streaming, eyes bulging, rose to the surface, plunging out into sunlight and air again, and began swimming. Dazed and winded, Roland hung on to the saddle horn and was dragged with it. There was little time or space to spare. The raft was fast approaching, swirling around, caught in the current which was racing towards the jaws of the ravine. Fortunately, Rajah was a strong swimmer and was making for the opposite bank.

But Wilk Price did not intend to let them get there alive. He was afraid to dive from the raft because he could not swim well. 'If I'm going, you're coming, too,' he shouted. He knelt to steady himself and took aim at the bounty hunter hanging to his swimming horse.

He fired, but as he did so Lucy kicked him in the back with all her force. 'Agh!' Wilk cried, and was pitched into the river, struggling to try to stay up as he was slowly swept away. He held out a pleading hand to Roland as he went past, but the former army captain could not have reached him even if he had wanted to. He watched him go. He was more interested in trying to pull Rajah's head around, to slow him up as the raft approached.

The bulky bunch of roped-together logs bumped into them and he reached out and caught the young woman as she slid into his arms. Jim looked into Lucy's jubilant face and could not restrain himself from kissing her as the valiant Rajah was given his head and swam strongly for the shore.

Roland gasped for breath and looking around saw Wilk Price, or his body, bobbing and twirling as it was gripped by the river's revenge and taken infallibly onwards towards the falls and certain death.

'Come on,' he shouted. 'Hang on, Lucy, or we'll all be going for a last ride.'

11

They dragged themselves out of the river, their clothes clinging to them. Lucy flopped down on a flat rock, watched the tall bounty hunter fondling his horse's mane and patting him while he loosened the cinch of the saddle. 'Rajah certainly saved our bacon,' he said, with a grin.

Shielded from the wind by the high crags, it was as hot as a bakehouse, the midday sun beating down out of a clear blue sky. 'If you don't object I'll dry my clothes,' she called and began to peel off her heavy sodden dress and stockings, tipping water from her bootees. 'Whoo, that was a narrow squeak. I thought my end had come when that ghastly Scud got his hands on me. Up till then I'd managed to evade anything awful happening.' She thought she had better reassure him on that account. 'You arrived in the nick of time.'

'Yeah. It was luck we just happened to get there.' A dimple in his cheek flickered as he stood in profile to her and removed Rajah's bridle. 'I could see you were about to suffer a fate worse than death. I didn't dare risk a shot with him on top of you. Never thought you'd have the presence of mind to pigstick him. Or maybe I did. Anyhow, Jesse made an easy target.'

'Thank goodness it's all over.' Lucy gave a sigh, as, looking at James Roland, her heart began to palpitate worse than it had when she was on the point of being raped. It was thumping in her chest now at the thought of what might occur, so alone here with this man. When he turned, his ice-blue eyes on her, his damp hair fallen over his brow, two weeks' growth of soft blond stubble on his lean jaws, she licked her lips and almost gulped. 'It's so hot,' she said, beginning to unbutton her bodice. 'I think I'll bathe. Do you mind? I need to wash away all this blood.'

He grinned again, wolfishly. 'Please yourself. I won't peep.' He turned away and pulled off his wet buckskin jacket to hang on the bough of a pine that had gained purchase in a cleft of the cliff. He slapped at his Stetson and propped that there, too. When he looked back Lucy had left her pantalets and bodice to dry on the rock and was squealing and splashing at herself in the calmer water of this inlet. Her naked body gleamed in the water like a sinuous fish as she swam back and forth. 'You having fun?'

'It's cold,' she cried, 'but it's beautiful to wash away all the dirt and trouble, to feel clean again. Why don't you come in?'

'Hm?' He considered this, studying her. 'You think that's wise?'

'Why not?'

'Waal, it's true I ain't bathed in a month or more. And I need to get outa these wet duds.' He ripped open his canvas, double-breasted shirt to reveal his lean and sun-bronzed upper body. He flicked away his bandanna, and hopped about to pull off his boots. Of custom, he glanced up around him at the cliffs, but the ravine was silent, just the sound of the rushing water and the falls further on. He met her eyes and began popping open the studs of his faded Levi jeans. 'Here I come,' he shouted and gave a whoop as he stepped out of them and dived in towards her.

'Oh, my God!' she cried, as he surfaced up beside her and grabbed her around her naked waist, pulling her slippery, wet body into him and rubbing himself up against her. 'I had forgotten what it was like.'

He wound his strong arms around her and dipped his head to nibble at the pert nipples of her bobbing breasts, so soft against his chest. 'Do I take it,' he murmured, 'I ain't the first?'

'Well, I can assure you it's not my custom to swim naked with strangers. I'm not easy, if that's what you mean.

But, yes, there have been one or two, or' — her grey eyes pronounced by their dark, distinct aureoles twinkled in the sunshine and smiled into his, as she raised his head — 'perhaps three . . . ?'

James Roland didn't need any more explanation or invitation. Their mouths met simultaneously and time and place was forgotten in a frenzy of kissing and caressing as he struggled to be at one with her . . .

A while later they crawled out on to the smooth, shelf of rock and lay exhausted, entwined in each other's arms, hearts pounding, as they dried off in the hot sun. 'I guess,' she whispered in his ear, 'I fall for the dangerous type.'

There seemed no need to speak further for some while, simply luxuriate in each other's touch and presence, as the sun began its fall and the shadows crept across. 'Jeez,' Roland sighed, 'what have I been missing all these years?'

'Yes,' she said, stroking him, 'with a *membrum virile* like this you should have made a lot of girls happy.'

'I've been out of circulation until recently. Two years in military prison.' He rolled onto his back and peered up at the cliffs, reaching for his Winchester to be closer at hand. 'I killed an officer senior to me.'

'You mean *you* were an officer?' Lucy propped herself on one elbow and stared at him. 'You know, I had an idea you were an educated man.'

'Self-educated, you could say. I never went to Westpoint or any of that stuff. I was commissioned in the field by Gen'ral Crook during the Sioux campaign. Guess I learned strategy where it counted, in battle. I eventually made captain. He was a major.'

'The man you killed?'

'Yup. It was over a woman. He insulted her. She was special to me. I hit him. He called me out. We had a duel, pistols at dawn, all that rigmarole. I aimed to wing him, but the damn fool moved to the side. Got him with a heart shot. Duelling is illegal these days. So I got court-martialled, stripped of my rank and sentenced to two years down the line.'

'So, when you came out you became a bounty hunter?'

'A man's got to do something. I guess it's better than being a stinkin' buffalo hunter. Sure, I've read a bit of Shakespeare, but my only real education has been knowing how to stay alive out in the wilderness and how to kill the enemy. So, I guess I'm well-qualified.'

'You plan to be a bounty hunter the rest of your life?' Lucy lay her head on his chest and ran her fingers up his ribcage. 'Or do you fancy settling down to a more normal life?'

'I've got a few dollars laid by. I've been thinking of going into ranching, maybe raise a family if I could meet the right type of woman. Might even give up spittin' baccy.'

'Hm?' Lucy raised herself and eyed him, quizzically, through her mass of damp hair. 'I'm not sure I'd make a good rancher's wife.'

'I haven't asked you.' He stroked her face, gently. 'I guess you've got a different life to me. We're just passing strangers really, ain't we?'

'I don't know, Jim.' Lucy sat up and shivered, reaching for her clothes. 'Come on, it's getting cold. My things are practically dry now.'

'Good. Right, you stay here, get a fire going. I'll swim Rajah across. I want to bury Hank and get his horse. There's a way down further back.' He pulled on his jeans and boots, flicked his hair out of his eyes. 'Then I want to bring those three stiffs across, Scud, Jesse and Fee. There's cash on 'em I can't miss.' He grinned at her and went to sling his saddle over Rajah. 'I should be back before dark. Will you be all right on your own?'

'Yes, go ahead.' Lucy was wriggling into her dry pantalets. 'I think I'll survive. What time will you expect your supper, sir? I believe you will have earned it. Oh, and by the way, James, thanks . . . for saving my life.'

'I think,' he said, 'you've thanked me adequately.'

* * *

By the time he got back, with three bobbing corpses roped one to the other as he crossed the river, Lucy Luffy had dried out their blankets and bedrolls, collected a good supply of dried kindling to last them the night. She had also erected a shelter roofed with pine boughs in a corner of the cove and generally made things shipshape, with a hearth of stones and a merry fire going to welcome him home in the dusk. Three trout she had caught with hair-pin, stick and string, were packed in clay and roasting in the ashes. She poured from the coffee pot into a tin mug and handed him the scalding brew. 'Here,' she said, 'you look like you could use this.'

'Hm,' he mused, as he sipped at it. 'Mighty impressive. You know, for a girl, you're really something.'

'Well, I'm not entirely empty-headed. I know more than books and bones. I rode round Colorado on a pony last winter in the snows on my own. It was difficult but I managed.'

He had strung his boots over his shoulders this time, so all he needed to do was dry his jeans over the fire. Then he joined her to pick voraciously at the trout, stuffing his mouth, too, with the flour bread she had made. He pulled a bottle from his saddle-bag, tipping whiskey into their cups and drawled, 'Bequeathed by Jesse. *Salud!*'

It was cosy and snug; their stomachs full and warmed by the whiskey, arms around each other as they lay in their blankets in front of the fire and looked out into the night's darkness and the smooth sheen of the river rolling by. Lucy was describing how the long-legged bear, the giant sloth, the camel and miniature horse would have roamed this land not so many years before, well, not in archaeological terms.

'Ever seen anything like this?' She took from her dress pocket the baby dinosaur's jawbone. 'It's far more exciting even than the mammoth we found in Indian Territory with lance heads embedded in it. That only went back to about 10,000 BC.'

And, then, she thought she had better fill him in about the men in her life, the cad of an army officer she had been besotted with when she was an impressionable young girl, the way he had used and deserted her, and how she had gone to Greece to forget and lose herself in her studies. The poet, Whitman, she had met in New York on her return, but who had turned out to be not all a man should be. And her expedition to Indian Territory when she had met the outlaw, Black Pete Bowen . . .

'Another dangerous character, huh?' Roland muttered, and offered her another drink of the whiskey. 'We might as well finish it up.'

Lucy screamed, sharply, and Jim stared in surprise, for rearing up out of the darkness on the other side of their fire a tall, ragged man appeared, his clothes damp and torn, his face scratched and bloody, his hair wild, aiming a long-barrelled Sharps at them.

'Put 'em up, you bastards.' Wilk Price squinted along the barrel at them. 'Surprise, surprise, eh? Thought I was dead, didn'cha?'

Jim Roland and Lucy were tongue-tied for a while, hardly able to believe this apparition. Then Lucy ventured, 'Before you kill us, would you explain how on earth you got back here?'

'How'n hell you think?' Wilk, with his thinning hair hanging over his cadaverous face, leered at her as he kept the Sharps aimed at Roland. 'I didn' go over the falls. I got caught on a snag and hauled myself out. I still had my rifle, as you see. I've been working my way back along the cliff face since then. It's been bloody hard, but I've made it.

Your camp-fire light kinda kept me going. An' here y'all are, snug as l'il bugs, thinkin' me dead and you all safe and sound. Hey, chuck me a bit of that corn-bread, sister. I'm starving.'

Lucy passed a piece to him and Wilk Price chewed at it, ravenously. 'You're shivering, Wilk,' she said, 'you must be frozen. Have a cup of this coffee. Look, I'll put the last of the whiskey in it.'

'Yeah?' One eye seemed to watch her while the other swivelled askance at Roland as Wilk reached out a shaking hand for the cup. 'Don't try no funny tricks.'

He crouched in front of them and supped at the brew, the Sharps cocked, its barrel aimed point-blank at the bounty hunter's chest. 'You, missy, are coming with me. Him,' — he tossed the cup away and shouted, squeezing the rifle's trigger — 'he can go to hell.'

As he took second pressure on the trigger Lucy hurled the pot of boiling coffee at him. 'Aagh!' he screamed, as it hit him full in the face. The rifle exploded, deafeningly, but the bullet went wild. Roland pulled his Lightning from beneath the blanket and emptied three shots in quick succession into Wilk, who hurtled back into the darkness.

Jim got to his feet and poked at Wilk's body with his boot to make sure he was dead. 'Well, that was nice of him to come back,' he drawled. 'Saves me the bother of going looking. That's another five hundred dollars in the kitty.'

12

It was an odd procession that arrived at the settlement of Green River, the bounty hunter, in his fringed buckskins and faded jeans, the lady in her outlaw's hat and long dress, both straddling horses which towed travois on which lay the corpses of four of the most wanted outlaws in that area of the West.

While Lucy booked them into the town hotel, Jim Roland laid the corpses of Jesse Greer, his son Scud, their cousins, Fee Fisher, and Wilk Price, on the sidewalk, scrawled their names large on cardboard placards placed on their chests, and had the town photographer take their picture for identification. Then he pushed through the gawping crowd to go and register his claim for their bounty with the town sheriff, to pay for their burial, and to inform the

Wyoming authorities of these facts by telegraph cable.

'Gosh,' Lucy sighed, as that afternoon she rolled into bed with Roland, 'isn't it wonderful to be able to stretch out on a real feather mattress?'

'It sure is.' He smiled, leaned on his elbows above her. 'Such joys are few and far between.'

When they went down for supper, however, she had a shock in store for her. 'Matt,' she cried, as she saw Professor Strangeways standing by the clerk's desk. 'Matt, is it really you?' She threw her arms around him to hug herself into him. 'I thought I was seeing a ghost.'

'No, I'm still alive,' he replied, his bandaged throat husky from the hanging. 'They brought me round, back from the dead, you might say. I was feeling pretty groggy for a day or two. But then I decided to get on a horse and come look for you.'

'You mean you rode all this way

through Indian country searching for me?'

'Well, they said something about Green River so I knew that was where they were heading for.'

The professor, his thick brush of greying hair hanging over his brow, looked faintly embarrassed as he released himself from her embrace and removed his spectacles. 'I was just enquiring here whether they had seen you. They said only a married couple under the name of Roland had booked in.'

'We ain't exactly tied the knot just yet.' James Roland grinned, as he offered his hand. 'It's great to see you, Matthew.'

'No doubt we are all indebted to you for saving Miss Luffy's life. To tell the truth I feared the worst.' The professor looked somewhat disconsolate as he added, 'It looks like the best man's won.'

'Come on, Matt, we're just going into supper.' Lucy hugged his arm. 'Get washed up and join us.'

There was a lot to talk about, but Jim Roland began to feel excluded as Matt and Lucy got their heads together. Scientific terms, geological data, writers he had never heard of, mutual acquaintances in Chicago.

'I can't wait to get back to the site,' Lucy cried, her eyes shining with animation. 'We'll get the stage back to Grand Junction in the morning, buy horses, cable Chicago, and ride back across the plateau to the dig.'

'Jim,' Matthew asked, 'could we pay you to be our guide and possibly protector?'

'Me? No!' Roland's eyes narrowed, as he pushed his coffee cup away. 'I got things to do. And, anyhow, two's company, three's a crowd.'

When they went back to bed later that night, the bounty hunter said, 'You know, I been listening to you two chattering away. Matt's the man you oughta marry, Lucy, not me.'

'Don't be silly,' she murmured, as she

kissed him. 'We're just good friends.'

'Waal,' he drawled, as he took her strongly in his arms, 'he ain't havin' you just yet.'

★ ★ ★

The rain was plodding down — two months later — turning Dutch John's street to a quagmire, as Lucy Luffy drove in beside Panos on his four-horse wagon. On the back of it was roped the gigantic skull of a brontosaurus.

Panos manoeuvred through the Hotchkiss guns, men and horses of the US Cavalry who had arrived to hunt down the Utes. 'We'll make an early start in the morning,' Lucy shouted, rain tipping from her hat, as she watched Panos stable the wagon and horses. 'You're sure you can get us to the railroad?'

'Sure, no problem.' The Greek smiled at her. 'Rain good. It make flowers grow. Come.' He beckoned her into his café. 'Tonight plenty ouzo. I cook you good.'

Mrs Panayotis fussed about her, drying her clothes, ushering her to a table, showing her the menu, and Lucy could not help but smile as she read, 'Foreribs of Cork . . . Apple Flitters . . . Live Bacon . . . Date with Tart.'

But she was worried: an eternal problem not unknown to millions of single girls. She was pregnant. Birth control was more or less non-existent. She had fallen for Jim Roland's child, but the bounty hunter had gone, north to Wyoming, pursuing another notorious criminal. Well, she thought, with a determined grimace, I'll just have to bring up the baby on my own.

'Wass the matter?' Panos was chiding, 'You no look very cheerful tonight. You worry 'bout dinosaur?'

'No,' she said, but faltered as she saw Professor Strangeways come through the doorway, his hat and slicker saturated with rain. 'Matt, what are you doing here? I thought you were staying back to guard the dig.'

'No. There's something I want to ask you.' He got hold of her arms and pulled her to her feet. 'I was worried in case you bump into that Roland fellow and he asks you first.'

'Why?' she protested. 'What?'

'Will you marry me, Lucy?'

'Matt, there's something I ought to tell you . . . '

'Don't worry about that. Mrs Panayotis, go get that preacher.' He hugged the girl to him. 'Lucy, please say you will.'

Lucy stared into his eyes, hesitating, then threw her arms around his shoulders. 'All right. I will.'

'Good.' Matt kissed her long and deep, then grinned at the Greeks, throwing down his wet slicker and seating himself at the table. 'Bring on the ouzo, Panos. Tonight I'm taking a drink. I'm starving, too. What's to eat?'

'Well, I was thinking of trying the Lover Sole with Paralysed Potatoes.'

Lucy hugged herself into his arms. 'But the Steak de Boot Wellington sounds good.'

'Mm,' the professor agreed, 'although it could be a mite tough.'

Afterword

Two years of fighting ended in 1881 when the Ute rebellion was put down by the US Army and the tribes were exiled from the White River reservation in Colorado to a bleak area of Utah.

Today, tourists flock to Dinosaur, near Dutch John, to marvel at the bones and fossils on display there, those that have not been removed to museums over the past century or more.

We do hope that you have enjoyed reading this large print book.

Did you know that all of our titles are available for purchase?

We publish a wide range of high quality large print books including:
Romances, Mysteries, Classics
General Fiction
Non Fiction and Westerns

Special interest titles available in large print are:
The Little Oxford Dictionary
Music Book, Song Book
Hymn Book, Service Book

Also available from us courtesy of Oxford University Press:
Young Readers' Dictionary
(large print edition)
Young Readers' Thesaurus
(large print edition)

For further information or a free brochure, please contact us at:
Ulverscroft Large Print Books Ltd.,
The Green, Bradgate Road, Anstey,
Leicester, LE7 7FU, England.
Tel: (00 44) **0116 236 4325**
Fax: (00 44) **0116 234 0205**

The minute Anderson landed at the remote Idaho rail station, he knew he'd find trouble. Some people out there wanted him dead. They'd started with a bushwhacking at the station house, and when that didn't work they kept right on trying. Just like he knew they would. When he woke up in a funeral parlour after a saloon gunfight, Anderson thought it couldn't get much worse, but pretty soon he realized he was wrong. From Idaho the trail led north into the Canadian wilderness, where a bunch of outlaw killers waited . . .

KILLER BROTHERS

Bill Williams

Ben Gleason, nearing the end of a long prison sentence for killing his father's murderer, is told that his younger brother has been sentenced to hang in five days' time. In a desperate attempt to save his brother, Ben escapes and starts the long journey home. He faces danger and temptation before his journey ends in a tragic discovery. Instead of being reunited with his family and the woman he hoped to marry, Ben experiences a living nightmare. Soon, he may well face the hangman's noose himself.

FIVE GUNS SOUTH

Dan Claymaker

They had robbed and pillaged their way through a whole territory by the time they hit the mountains. But the five raiders, led by Luke Quantril, were saving their cruellest heist for the quiet town of Bandyrock. Here, they held the town brutally to ransome until they had drained it of every last dollar, before heading for the border with trailed hostages at their mercy. Then it was left to Sheriff Connell and a greenhorn posse to pursue the raiders across the searing desert . . .

STOLEN HORSES

John Dyson

Young wrangler Quince Simms is well pleased when he lands a job tending the sixty-horse remuda of Big John Durham. But Quince falls for the rancher's daughter, Marie, and when his boyhood pal, the fast-shooting dude Lance Silverlight arrives on the scene, it's a recipe for disaster! Not only does the handsome Lance sweet-talk Marie into the hay, but he also heads for the border, taking the rancher's remuda with him. Now it's up to Quince to strap on his Colt and cross the Rio Grande in pursuit of the stolen horses . . .

THE BLADON BUNCH

Tom Benson

The bank at Pyke's Crossing seemed an easy target and Will Bladon and his sons struck ruthlessly. But after a killing and a wild chase, they learned a bitter lesson — they needed someone who could plan things and show them how to get around banks' defences. Josh Abbot, a scruffy character, became the brains that directed the Bladon bunch. An out-of-work cowpoke and a greedy marshal were both after the rewards on offer. The Bladons were being hunted, and it would end in a deadly shoot-out.